His voice whispered in her head

Julia repeated his name, praying that somehow that could make Linc materialize there before her. For the first time in weeks she closed her eyes and pictured his face. Not the face that had been lined with anger and red with rage as he argued with her. Not the face of the man who silently drank his coffee each morning before work and barely spoke to her. Not the face of the man who'd stridden from the house the other night.

She saw the boy she'd fallen in love with back in high school. The boy she'd stayed up late with cramming for finals in college. The man whose face shone in completion as he made love to her.

Dear Reader,

Whenever a catastrophe strikes, the media are quick to descend, and we often see events as they happen. During the Sago Mine disaster in 2006, one picture of a woman crumbling into tears touched my heart. I wanted to put my arms around her and comfort her. She stayed with me over the next few days and I wondered about her, about her story.

She developed into Julia. I could see that Julia cared deeply—it was etched into the pain on her face in that picture. Linc soon appeared, and I knew their story was powerful. From there the words and images came—of a tough breed of people who go to work each day and risk their lives. And while I can't understand how they can bear to let their loved ones go, I know many families do just that each and every day. Julia and Linc travel a rough road and have to—literally—try to move a mountain in healing their love. I hope you enjoy reading their story as much as I have appreciated writing it.

I love to hear from readers. Please feel free to contact me at angelsmits@q.com or at P.O. Box 63202, Colorado Springs, CO 80962-3202. Follow me on Facebook or Twitter, as well.

Happy reading!

Angel Smits

A Message for Julia
Angel Smits

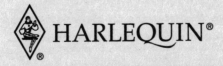

HARLEQUIN®

TORONTO • NEW YORK • LONDON
AMSTERDAM • PARIS • SYDNEY • HAMBURG
STOCKHOLM • ATHENS • TOKYO • MILAN • MADRID
PRAGUE • WARSAW • BUDAPEST • AUCKLAND

Recycling programs
for this product may
not exist in your area.

ISBN-13: 978-0-373-71679-1

A MESSAGE FOR JULIA

www.eHarlequin.com

Printed in U.S.A.

ABOUT THE AUTHOR

Angel Smits's background as a geriatric social worker has given her a glimpse into many varied lives and generations. She often finds her characters and stories in the people she's met. A people watcher, she is frequently at the mall or nearby bookstore simply observing all the craziness—especially during Christmas, where there's so much to see. Angel has received Romance Writers of America's Golden Heart Award and has previously published two paranormal romances and several nonfiction articles. *A Message for Julia* is her first book for Harlequin Superromance. Angel lives in Colorado with her husband and soon-to-be-moving-out son and daughter. The cat and dog plan to stay.

For all the men who go to work each day
and face the danger, and the women
who kiss them goodbye and let them go.

Pat, you would have loved this one.
The mimosas are on me.

And Ron. Simply—thank you!

CHAPTER ONE

Thursday Afternoon, 3:00 p.m.

NORMALLY THE SMELL OF CHALK dust comforted Julia Holmes, but not today. Maybe never again.

Shaking her head, she turned back to the blackboard and finished erasing the scrawled lessons, wishing she could erase the day's events just as easily.

The letter of reprimand from the school board lay on her desk, as disturbing to her peace of mind as the empty seat in the second row.

She'd only been trying to help.

Ryan Sinclair, one of her students, had dropped out of school last week to take a job at the mine. She'd tried to talk some sense into him. He was bright and talented with too much potential to be stuck working in a coal mine the rest of his life. The school board hadn't appreciated her "meddling" as they called it, and the letter on her desk told her so quite clearly.

Her presence was requested at tomorrow night's school-board meeting. She swallowed the lump of apprehension that threatened to choke her.

A cough in the doorway pulled her out of her thoughts. Julia turned to see Missy Watson standing there. The girl had been quiet in class today, and Julia was surprised to see tears in her eyes now. "Missy? Are you okay?" She stepped around to the front of the desk.

A sob ripped from Missy's throat. Dropping the eraser, Julia hurried to her. Tears cut pale tracks in her too-heavy makeup.

"What's the matter?" Julia spoke softly, carefully, laying a hand on her student's arm.

"It's…it's all my fault."

"What's your fault?"

"The whole mess you're in. With Ryan."

Understanding dawned. Julia gently squeezed the arm she held. "It's okay, Missy." Obviously talk had gotten around about the reprimand she'd received. Or, at the very least, the tongue-lashing the principal had given her. She'd known last week that news of Ryan's father's blowup had been all over the school.

All because she'd cared.

"No, it's not." Missy dissolved into tears again. "I didn't really want him to leave. But…but…"

Julia's heart ached for the girl. She remembered all too clearly being seventeen and feeling as if the world rested on your every decision.

Despite the warnings against touching students, Julia slipped her arms around Missy's slim shoulders.

"I teased him." Missy's voice wobbled. "He asked me to the prom and I said no." The last word was more a wail than anything.

"Oh, I'm sure he recovered from that." Teenagers and dating. It was a minefield, and while Julia wanted to help Missy, she knew better than to venture in too far. Besides, she wasn't exactly qualified to give advice about love. She hastily put thoughts of her own marriage out of her mind.

"No. I…I told him I didn't want to date *boys*. I wanted to go out with a *man*. But that's not true. I really like him."

"Oh, dear." Julia could imagine the slap in the face those words had been.

"It's not your fault he left school. It's mine." She sobbed into Julia's collar. "And now you're in trouble and might lose your job."

Missy's guilt seemed all too powerful right then. Julia knew she needed to ease the girl's tears, though she hoped Missy had learned something from this. Maybe she'd think twice before spouting off hurtful remarks in the future. "I'm not going to lose my job." Julia wasn't sure who needed to believe it more, her or Missy.

"You're not?" Missy pulled back and looked up. "Oh, thank goodness. You're the best teacher. I'm doing lousy in all my other classes."

She wasn't doing that well in this one, either, but Julia left that unsaid. Missy hastily wiped her face. Smudges of black mascara ringed her damp blue eyes.

"To be honest, Missy, I'd do it again." And she would. "Sometimes you have to fight for the things you care about."

Missy seemed to consider that. "So, you think I should fight for Ryan?"

"Well…" Julia wasn't getting sucked in again. She'd already done enough damage by trying to give a kid advice. "That's up to you. Just think about it."

"I will. Thanks, Mrs. Holmes. You're the best."

Before Julia could say anything more, Missy headed to the door and probably straight to the restroom to fix her makeup. Ah, the resilience of youth.

Julia returned to her desk and sank into her chair, wishing she were as resilient as Missy. She stared at the letter, not really seeing it, not needing to read the words. Despite what she'd told Missy, she *could* lose her job.

She looked out the window of her classroom. From the third floor, she could see most of Parilton, Pennsylvania, with its clapboard houses and tree-lined streets. The dark silhouette of the Winding Trail Mine sat at the edge of town, mother hen and vulture all in one. Just as it overshadowed the town, it touched every life in Parilton, including hers.

Her husband, Linc, was working up there today, as he'd been, on and off, for several weeks. New equipment going in meant inspection after inspection, all his responsibility. It was another in a long list of things that kept him away from home.

She'd hardly seen him in weeks, it seemed. She missed him, and that knowledge bothered her more than she wanted it to. What was worse was the realization that she had to talk to Linc about the letter. About the whole mess.

She'd finally have to tell him about the job change she'd made last month. She'd meant to tell him about it earlier but had never quite found the right moment. She knew she should have tried harder—waited up when he came in late, woken him before she left in the morning, or found a way to meet for lunch.

But she hadn't quite figured out what to say, or how to explain it to him. She didn't even understand it herself. And since they barely spoke these days anyway, keeping silent was just easier.

Until today, she'd thought it was the right decision.

Friday Morning, 5:30 a.m.

THE ALARM CLATTERED at oh-dark-thirty. Julia rolled over and smacked the off button, hoping she'd permanently disabled the thing. She opened one eyelid then slammed it shut again

She did *not* want to face today.

Linc's even breathing broke the quiet of the room, and she turned to look at him in the dim morning light. She'd tried to stay awake last night to talk to him, but the long hours and stress had taken their toll. Either she had become so used to Linc coming in late, or he was getting better at being quiet.

Maybe she'd wait until tomorrow, when they were both home and not working, to tell him. *After* she knew the results of tonight's meeting. No, that would only make matters worse.

"Hey," she said softly and waited. No answer. She said it again, louder.

"You say something?" he mumbled.

"Yeah. Are you awake?" She waited for him to wake enough to understand what she was saying. He didn't stir and she knew she'd lost the battle. Rather than try again, Julia climbed out of bed, throwing the covers aside and silently hoping the cool air would startle him awake.

For a long moment, Julia stared down at the mussed bed and grieved the loss of the days when she'd wake him early for an entirely different purpose. With a sigh, she abandoned those thoughts and headed downstairs to make breakfast. She needed something to do to keep her mind and hands busy.

She threw on her robe, letting it hang open, the belt trailing behind. What was the point of looking present-able when she was alone with no one to appreciate her? She shook her head; she needed coffee to chase away the pity party in her mind.

Bitter caffeine, tempered by sugar and cream, ca-ressed her tongue. She stood at the kitchen window and gazed over the rim of her coffee cup at the house across the street. The neighbors were a young couple. All their windows were still dark. Were they asleep? Or had morning come for them as well and their bed was still cozy and inviting? She closed her eyes...wishing.

Wishing for what?

For those early days of her marriage before every moment was a struggle? The days before they'd started talking about a family?

She heard the footstep an instant before warm, strong arms stole around her waist.

"You were saying something?" Linc's voice was thick with sleep, but she sighed in relief. He'd heard her. On some level he'd been listening.

"Yeah."

He waited. She took a deep breath.

"I...I quit my job at the elementary school," she finally whispered.

Linc went absolutely still against her. Julia wasn't even sure she felt him breathing.

"What? Why?" He came around to face her. She missed the warmth he'd provided. She looked up at him. He frowned and leaned back against the counter, crossing his arms over his bare chest. She couldn't help but drink in the view of the lightly tanned plains and valleys sprinkled with dark hair. The jeans he'd hastily thrown on hung low on his hips.

But the warmth that had been in his body didn't show on his face. She shivered and looked down at her coffee. "I can't do it anymore."

"Can't do what? Teach?"

"No. Not teach. I have another job. I can't be around the little ones." Her voice broke on the last words.

"Another job? Where?"

Now she knew she had to look at him. "I've been teaching at the high school for the past month. I'm subbing for an English teacher who's out on maternity leave."

His frown deepened and a flush swept up his face. "A month?" He moved away from the counter and paced away from her. "When were you going to tell me?"

She shrugged. "I don't know. I didn't intend *not* to tell you. I just didn't know how to bring it up. You're so busy—"

"That's no excuse."

"I know that."

The stiff way he held himself told her she'd hit a

nerve. They'd never kept secrets before—before last fall when the whole world had fallen apart.

"There's more," Julia said softly, staring out the window instead of at Linc's bare chest. She wished he owned a robe. Maybe she'd get him one for Christmas. Why was she thinking about that now? She knew she was avoiding this, avoiding talking to him. She didn't want to discuss the hurt that had never gone away.

"Oh, this should be good."

His sarcasm irritated her. He'd been sarcastic a lot lately. "Stop it." She stepped farther away from him. "I don't want to argue again. I know I should have told you sooner and I'm sorry about that, but what's done is done," she said, throwing his favorite phrase back at him. "I don't know how much longer I'll have this job." Her voice broke, but she refused to give in to her emotions. Not now.

"What does that mean?" At least the sarcasm was gone.

She swallowed hard. "Yesterday I…I received a letter of reprimand from the school board. They…they are reviewing my contract at tonight's meeting." This time there was no hiding the hurt in her voice. She didn't want his pity. She just wanted him to listen for a change.

"Why?" He drew the word out.

"I tried to convince one of the boys not to quit school to work in the mine. He was only a few months away from graduating." Her voice was soft. "His father went to the school board—but not before reaming me out, of course."

"Oh, great. Are you crazy? That mine is the lifeblood

of this town. Every person here depends on it." Linc
ran a hand through his hair and walked over to the cof-
feemaker. He poured himself a cup and took his time
taking that first sip.

"I know that."

He closed his eyes as if to savor his coffee, or to
ignore her. "So you're trying to go up against the mine
management. It was Ryan Sinclair, wasn't it?"

"You heard about it?"

"Half the town heard Jack Sinclair running off at the
mouth. I didn't know he was talking about you. Ryan's
working up at the mine now. I gather your little talk
didn't convince him."

"No." She winced. She'd always found it hard to
admit her failures.

The kitchen fell silent, heavy with unsaid words as
they both nursed cooling cups of coffee.

WHO WAS THIS WOMAN standing in his kitchen? Linc
couldn't help but stare at Julia.

She'd been edgy lately and he'd known something
was wrong. But he'd learned years ago not to push her.
Right now she looked a mess—a just-waking-up-in-the-
morning mess—but still a mess. Her hair was mussed
and her robe hung open to show the shorts and T-shirt
she'd slept in. He let his gaze linger on her curves…
wishing…

When the hell had they grown so far apart that he
couldn't even touch his wife when he wanted to?

Like now.

"You could—" She stepped toward him. "Could you

put something about how it's not safe for kids to work in the mines in your report?"

He stared at her, incredulous. "No."

"Why not?"

His anger surprised him. She'd always had her causes and another thing he'd learned was to take cover when she started talking about one of them. Why couldn't they have a conversation anymore without one of them getting angry? He forced himself to focus, to tamp down his reaction. "For one, I'm not willing to risk my career for someone else's problem. And this isn't your business. One of us has to keep working and feed us."

"And two?" she bit out.

"I don't agree with you. Ryan is old enough to make his own decisions.

"He's only seventeen."

"When I was seventeen, I was on my own. At least he has parents to turn to, which he did."

"They don't understand—"

"No, Julia. *You* don't understand. Ever since…since…last fall…" His voice wavered, but he quickly caught himself. "You want to fix everyone else's life. Take care of every lost soul that crosses your path." He stepped closer to her, lowering his voice, hoping to ease the tension between them. "Maybe you should focus on your own problems and your own life for a change."

"That's not fair."

"Whoever told you life was fair? It sure as hell wasn't me."

He closed his eyes for an instant trying to clear his mind. His life had never been even close to fair. But what bothered him most was the fact she'd kept all of this—her new job and this crisis—a secret from him. They'd never had secrets.

When he'd first heard Jack, he realized now, some part of his brain had thought it sounded like Julia. But he'd dismissed it because he'd thought she was still teaching at the elementary school. Now he wasn't as shocked as he should be. "Julia, don't do this."

"Don't do what?" She actually sounded surprised.

"This. It's not your battle."

"I disagree." She stomped across the kitchen and stared out the back window.

The distance between them was too great. He had to find a way across it. "Tell me why you left the elementary school." He did *not* want to start this conversation, but it now seemed inevitable.

"I couldn't do it. Because…it…it just wasn't for me." She fidgeted with the belt of her robe.

Linc hated seeing the forlorn look on her face. He ached to pick her up, carry her away and fix it all. He also knew she'd resist that and probably deck him in the process. "I can be there tonight."

She looked up, and he thought she was going to smile. He held his breath, waiting. He couldn't remember the last time she'd truly smiled.

"But I'm not promising anything else." He couldn't do more than that.

She nodded and turned away again.

Linc went back upstairs, back to bed for a couple hours. He wished she'd join him, but he knew better.

She'd have to call in sick to work and she took her commitments seriously—too seriously sometimes.

The sheets were too damned cold.

CHAPTER TWO

Friday Evening, 7:00 p.m.

THE CAFETERIA WAS FULL, but not so full that it was intimidating. Julia looked around. She knew most of these people, some by name but more by face.

The six-member school board sat up front at a couple of the lunch tables that had been turned sideways. The twenty or so other people sat at tables where her students usually hung out laughing and eating lunch. It was a small town. A relatively small school. Nothing fancy.

A few more people filed in and Julia leaned forward. Where was he? Her heart sank. She didn't want to think that Linc had broken his promise, but he did have a habit of getting caught up in work at times and forgetting things—like dinner.

The board had reviewed the budget, rehashed the booth at the county fair and had just started to go over the upcoming end-of-year graduation activities when the door creaked open.

Julia fought her smile. She'd always prided herself on being independent. She didn't want people to think she was one of those women who couldn't survive without a man. But knowing that Linc had come to support her made something inside her shift, something warm.

Maybe she wouldn't have to do this alone anymore. He wound his way into the room and took the seat beside her.

After another ten minutes, the meeting seemed to be winding down. Julia fought not to get her hopes up. Maybe they'd forget about her contract.

"One final item," a woman at the end of the table said. Julia craned her neck to see. She recognized her. She knew Shirley Wise from various events as well as from when she'd interviewed for the job at the high school.

"Is Julia Holmes here?" Shirley looked directly at her.

"I'm here." Julia remained seated and Linc nudged her with his elbow.

"Stand up," he muttered.

Julia frowned at him, but stood rather than have anyone around them hear her argue.

"We've reviewed your contract and the letter of reprimand." Shirley looked over her half glasses at Julia. "Both will stand, barring any further incidents. Thank you, everyone—"

That was it? She wasn't going to get the chance to speak? People around her looked confused and disapproving. Many probably already knew what had happened, others were totally clueless and were thinking the worst of her. Julia wanted to have her chance to defend herself and her actions.

"Julia, shhh," Linc said softly. He knew her too well, but he should also know she wasn't going to back down.

"I'd like to have my say."

"It won't make a difference."

Shocked, she turned to stare down at him. What did he mean it wouldn't make a difference? To him? To the school board? To her?

Before she could recover and respond to Shirley, the crowd stood and the board members were heading to the door. Her heart sank and her anger rose. She glared at Linc, knowing disappointment fueled her ire.

She was a good teacher, she knew that. She'd worked so hard for and at this job. She loved her students. She stared at Linc. He didn't meet her gaze. He was chatting with the woman beside him, making casual conversation about the weather. Totally unaware that his actions were what hurt the most.

Suddenly, she realized he no longer believed in her.

LINC KNEW HE WAS in serious trouble, knew from a lifetime of experience and seven years of living with Julia that he was in deep. What he didn't know was how to fix it. The helplessness he felt had become familiar over the past several months. He knew he should face it head-on, but instead, he let the woman beside him go on and on about the dry spell they were having. He couldn't have cared less about the weather.

The crowd thinned, and he waited for Julia to head to the door. He turned to look at her and immediately regretted the impulse. She was ticked, all right.

But even worse was the pain he saw lurking behind the anger in her eyes. His heart sank. Maybe there was no fixing any of this.

They drove home separately. He followed her SUV

in his truck. Her taillights burned red as they drove through town where few streetlights had come on. In the distance, the glow of the mine created a halo on the horizon. His mind wandered to the work he had to get done up there tomorrow.

He suddenly felt very tired.

Linc pulled in beside her in the garage. Even before he'd opened his door, she was out of her car and the force of her door slamming shook the entire vehicle. She stomped up the two steps to the house and slammed that door, too.

Linc just sat there staring at the closed door. He briefly wondered if she'd locked him out. He cursed. He did *not* want to go into that house. If he did, what would he say? What would she say?

He knew it would take a while for her to cool down. Maybe he should just spend the night here in the truck. It wouldn't be the first time.

Long moments passed. Long silent moments. Slowly, the door opened. Julia stood there in the opening, the kitchen light haloing her just as the mine's lights had haloed the skyline earlier.

He couldn't see her features clearly in the shadow, but her arms were crossed over her chest. She stood facing him, probably glaring at him, for a minute, then she spun on her heel. At least she didn't slam the door this time but he knew he was no more welcome now than he had been before.

Well, hell, he cursed silently. He'd spent the past seven months walking on eggshells around her, being cautious of her feelings, trying to fix everything. Why did he always have to be the good guy?

He shoved the truck door open, smacking it into the side of her car, not caring if he left a ding, not caring about anything all of a sudden. He walked slowly into the house, closing the door and deliberately locking it up for the night as he always did.

Finally, he faced his wife. She stood by the window, staring out at the backyard. He walked over to the fridge and opened it, the light harsh in the growing shadows, and grabbed a beer. The *sizzle-pop* as he broke the seal was loud. His swallow seemed loud in his head, but probably wasn't. The drink sat heavy in his gut.

"Go ahead, get it over with." He sighed and took another painful gulp. Her silence tore through the night and through him.

JULIA WANTED TO HIT HIM. Where that reaction came from she didn't know, but suddenly she realized how far apart they'd grown. How distant they were. For the first time in all the years they'd been married, she doubted they'd be together forever. All these painful months, she'd thought they'd find their way back to each other. But she couldn't do this anymore, and apparently neither could he.

Linc walked over to the trash and tossed the empty beer bottle inside. He headed for the doorway, but stopped when he reached it. His back was to her, and the way he braced his shoulders told her he was far from done.

She was right. He didn't turn around but the voice that came from his throat was nothing like she'd ever heard before. It tore at her heart. "Maybe God was being kind when he took the baby away." He took a few more steps. "Maybe we weren't ever supposed to be a family."

He went into the living room and she stood there, as frozen as if he'd slapped her. Linc had hurt her before, but this was worse than anything she'd experienced. Not only because he'd set out to hurt her. But because he had wounded himself in the same instant he'd lashed out at her.

He was halfway to the front door before she was able to speak. "Why did you even bother coming tonight?" She followed him. "Shushing me isn't being exactly supportive."

"Support? Is that all you want from me? Just my support?" He said the last word as if it left a bad taste in his mouth. "I went to make sure you didn't screw up and get fired. And you would have if you'd opened your mouth."

"You don't know that."

"Don't I? Don't you?"

Anger and pain crashed through her. "Damn you, Linc. I…I hate you." The words burst out, driven by the frustration that had built over the past seven months.

He turned back to face her, his hand curling around the doorknob. "That makes two of us."

He didn't say any more, but the spark of fury that flashed in his eyes hurt. Something drove her to want to hurt him back. "I'm leaving. I can't do this anymore."

"Can't do what?" He let go of the knob, all six-feet-two inches of him moving to within touching distance. "Keep working at our marriage?"

Julia almost reached out to him, but couldn't seem

to remember how. For months they'd been so distant, she'd forgotten what it felt like to be comfortable with him. An ache grew inside and she just wanted it all to go away.

"I'd say you quit working at it a long time ago." Linc glared at her. "You didn't even tell me you'd left your job a month ago!"

"I intended to tell you."

"Yeah, right." He moved away again.

"Oh, and you're any better?" She stomped toward him. "You won't even discuss going to see a fertility specialist. I want a *family,* Linc."

"And I'd be happy just to have a wife at this point." His breath came in deep gulps. The air in the room crackled with anger. With frustration. With wanting something—anything else.

The hardness in his eyes wasn't something Julia had ever seen before. He was silent so long that she turned back to the kitchen.

His voice came out so softly, she'd have missed it if she'd gone any farther. "You've already left me," he whispered.

She heard the door open and spun around to watch him disappear into the shadows of the front porch.

His words sounded final. Permanent. Wrong.

But wasn't that what she wanted, what she needed to get herself and her life back on track? Lifting her chin, Julia stared after him, then turned on her heel and hurried to the bedroom.

She yanked an overnight bag from the closet and

shoved a change of clothes, toiletries and little else into it. "Damn you, Linc," she muttered.

Why didn't he come back into the house? Was he just going to let her go? She didn't hear the roar of his truck's engine, so she knew he was still here.

Fine, if that's how he wanted it, she'd leave.

She grabbed her purse and her car keys and ran, as best she could with the suitcase in her hand, back to the garage. Her car still pinged, cooling from her trip home. The dome light washed out the open door, almost welcoming. The starter ground painfully and her tires squealed on the pavement.

She tried not to look back. She simply glanced in the rearview mirror, catching a final, fleeting look at the tiny house she loved so much. She tore her gaze away. All her dreams lay back there, shattered and lost.

A sob broke loose from her throat, and Julia let it settle in the night air. Where was she going? What was she supposed to do now? There wasn't a single person in this godforsaken town she could turn to.

She drove to the edge of town, out near the interstate where a few hotels sat scattered along the worn highway. The Holiday Inn was the first one she reached, and she checked in.

Nothing was ever going to be the same again.

Sunday Afternoon, 5:30 p.m.

LINC DOUBTED THERE had ever been a game of chess played anywhere near the Chess Club. But the picture of a Black Queen chess piece looked cool on the old tavern sign. He stepped inside, blinking as his eyes adjusted to the sudden darkness.

Miners came here after every shift. Since moving here, he'd gotten into the habit of stopping in once or twice a week to meet up with some of the guys. He'd started doing it to try to build relationships. Now, he just needed company.

Art and Luther, old men who'd put in their time at the mines and now enjoyed retirement, sat in their usual seats at the end of the bar. Grant, the owner, stood behind the bar, perpetually polishing glasses. It all felt so normal.

Linc was the one out of kilter. He claimed a barstool and ordered a beer. He'd downed half of it before a hand clapped him on the shoulder.

"Hey, buddy. Where the hell you been?" Mark Thompson, a miner he'd become friends with since he'd started coming here, smiled at him. He and Mark had developed a friendship of sorts, based mainly on their love of football and failure at darts. Mark climbed up on the barstool beside him and ordered a repeat of Linc's drink.

"Been busy." Linc had thought he wanted someone to talk to, anything but the silence of the house without Julia, but now he realized that talking was one thing he didn't want to do.

"Yeah, I heard about what happened at the meeting. Bet your wife is ticked."

That was putting it mildly. "Yeah." He took another deep swallow of his beer.

"She'll get over it. You up for a game?" Mark tilted his head toward the dartboard. Linc just shook his head.

"Too bad. I was in the mood to kick your butt." Mark drank his own beer with a smile.

They sat in silence for a long while. Linc had just finished his beer when the door opened. His gaze met Mark's in the mirror. Darlene sauntered in. Mark's eyes lit up while Linc groaned. He wasn't up for her and her shenanigans. She knew Mark had a thing for her, and every time Linc came in she played this stupid game of coming on to him. All to make Mark jealous.

"Hey, guys." She took the stool on the opposite side of Linc. He didn't even look at her, but watched Mark eyeballing her in the mirror. He should just get up and leave, but going back to the empty house didn't appeal to him at all.

"Hey, Grant, give me another one."

"I heard some news." Darlene leaned over to Linc, staring straight into his eyes. "I hear your wife tore out of your driveway the other night and hasn't been back since." She gently rested her hand on his forearm as though to comfort him, but Linc felt she wanted more.

He swallowed hard, but didn't look at her. He did not need this. Grant set the beer in front of him and he resisted the urge to drain the glass. "Who've you been talking to?"

"Oh, people around." She grinned, as if she knew she held a morsel of truth.

"That true?" Mark sounded upset by the news. Linc didn't know if it was because he hadn't told him, or because now he saw Linc as a real threat to his chances with Darlene.

"We just had a fight," Linc said through clenched

teeth. "We'll be fine." He wondered if they knew he was lying.

"That's not what people are saying." Darlene smiled too brightly. She leaned against him now, her breast brushing against his arm so slightly it could almost have been an accident. He swallowed hard and mentally cursed. This wasn't happening. He took another swig of his beer and nonchalantly scooted away from her.

Mark leaned forward, trying to get Darlene's attention. "What's wrong with you, girl? Can't you see the man's in no mood for your company?"

"This isn't any of your business." She leaned forward, pressing against Linc more deliberately this time.

Darlene wasn't a bad person, and in another life he might actually have been attracted to her.

Anger pulsed through him. In all the years he'd been with Julia, he'd been faithful to her. He'd never cheated, never even thought about it. And where had that gotten him? Seven years of marriage down the tubes and an empty house waiting for him.

He looked at Darlene. What if…

"I'm going home." He stood and Darlene climbed down from the stool. "Alone." He headed to the door and didn't bother looking back. He knew there wasn't anyone he wanted except Julia. And he might spend the rest of his life wanting something he couldn't have.

For five days, Linc waited for Julia to come back. He went to work every morning, expecting her to be there when he returned each night. Her spot in the garage remained tauntingly empty.

He called everyone they knew—and that was damned

few people here in town. No one had heard from her. She hadn't contacted anyone, except to call in sick to work.

On Wednesday night he found the light on the answering machine blinking when he walked in the door. He pushed Play and Julia's voice filled the house, banishing the shadows that threatened to take over. He held his breath as he listened.

"Linc, I'll be by tomorrow afternoon to pick up the rest of my things." That was it. Nothing more.

He played the message five times before grabbing the machine and throwing it across the room. It shattered against the dining-room wall. He felt only marginally better.

He called her cell phone—again. It went straight to voice mail, which told him she'd turned it off. There was nothing else he could do.

Except wait.

He cursed and grabbed a beer from the fridge. Damn it all. He needed oblivion. And he certainly didn't need half the town watching him find it.

By Thursday, when he pulled into the dirt parking lot of the Winding Trail Mine ten minutes early to shadow the afternoon shift, he was exhausted.

He wanted to finish this job and get home in time to catch Julia. He needed to do something—talk to her—anything to figure out how to make things better. There was too much anger between them and he didn't like it. To be honest, he was downright sick of it. They were facing some tough decisions and he just wanted it done.

Linc had always been the type who yanked off a bandage. It hurt like hell but then it was over. None of this slow, methodical agony. If his marriage was going to end, he wanted that flash of pain, not this ongoing hurt.

Shaking his head, he tried to clear his mind of all those thoughts. He had a job to do and it required focus. He got out of the truck and reached into the bed to grab his gear before mounting the rough wooden steps to the mine office.

The faded, worn building, the size of a double-wide trailer, had two shabby offices in front and a larger room beyond. In the back room, which served as a locker room, he met up with the crew he'd been assigned to shadow.

Six men looked up when he walked in. They were nearly finished dressing in their long johns, flannel shirts and coveralls. Now that he was here, they would go underground.

Linc hustled to dress as they introduced themselves. He recognized Gabe Wise, the crew chief, from his previous visit. Linc immediately realized why the older man was in charge. They were a young crew and Gabe had nearly twenty years experience.

Robert Hastings, a gruff man who looked to be in his early forties, simply nodded when Linc acknowledged him. Ah, a man of few words. Then there were brothers Michael and Ryan Sinclair. He already knew them. All too well. The fight with Julia after the school-board meeting came back to him. What a mess.

As long as Ryan was old enough, there wasn't

anything Linc could do. The law said he only had to stay in school until he was sixteen.

At least Ryan was on a crew with his older brother who could keep an eye on him.

Linc guessed the other members of the group, Casey McGuire and Zach Hayes, were in their late twenties. Obviously friends, they joked with the rest of the men but kept just enough apart to show they weren't yet a cohesive team.

All dressed and accounted for, they donned hard hats, clipped fresh batteries to their tool belts and climbed aboard the transport—a flatbed cart they called a man-trap. Linc hefted his backpack, his unofficial briefcase for trips down into the mines, up on his shoulder. Passing into the yawning mouth of the mine, he cringed. God, he hated this part. His heart and breath hitched at the thought of the tons of rock over his head. A normal reaction, he knew, but still he felt it tight in his gut.

The heavy damp scent of earth surrounded him. It felt as if he was stepping into a half-dug grave. That was one reason why he was an inspector and not a workaday miner. His goal was to keep these men safe—unlike the mine inspectors of old who'd failed his father.

The instant they were inside, Linc's gaze darted around, scanning the low ceiling, the thick walls and the equipment they passed. There were several things he wanted to examine more closely on the trip out. But on the whole, he'd seen worse.

Nearly half an hour later, Gabe spoke. "Here we are." His voice soaked into the dark walls. He jumped from the transport as deftly as a man half his age and the others followed, forming a line that seemed preordained. They finished the last few yards on foot.

Each man went to his position as Linc watched, taking mental and written notes. The machines roared to life as the crew started to dig for the rich, black coal. The engines' noise prevented conversation, but the miners managed to communicate through gestures and the simple fact that they knew their jobs and their places.

With the light from his hard hat guiding him, Linc moved around the cavern, examining, checking and letting his skeptical mind search for any indication of sloppiness or intentional violations. A loud metallic *chink* shattered the din. The pitch of the digger's engines changed and Linc spun around.

The grinding of metal on metal told them the cutting black had hit something abnormal.

Shit. Gabe looked to the right wall and Linc followed his line of sight but couldn't see anything. Suddenly, the roar around them drowned out even the engines' noise. Rock tumbled down the face they'd been digging. Linc saw rather than heard Gabe's command, "Run!"

Robert scrambled off the loader. Mike grabbed Ryan's arm in a grip that Linc knew had to be painful. Gabe waited until all his men were ahead of him. Casey and Zach were to his left, not moving. Why weren't they rushing to the exit?

Linc turned and his gaze met Gabe's. Together, they saw that Casey's left leg was trapped beneath the caterpillar track of the scoop. *Damn*.

Running the few feet, Linc joined Gabe and Robert

on the side of the machine. The three of them pushed but the heavy piece of equipment barely budged. Again they pushed. Again it barely moved.

Luckily, as they worked to free Casey, no more shale fell around them. But that was no guarantee it wouldn't bury them before they took their next dust-laden breath.

Linc didn't hear the others approach, but he felt their presence beside him. Gabe set the pace with an even rhythm and counted it off. On three they all pushed. Ryan and Mike's young muscle added to theirs was just enough to tip over the machine.

Casey grimaced, but he clenched his jaw as he fought crying out. His pain was palpable in the chamber with them. Looking lower, Linc realized Casey's leg was badly mangled.

The roar returned. Gabe waved them on as he shoved his shoulder under Casey's armpit.

Zach took the other side. "Let's get the hell out of here."

Together they half carried, half dragged the injured man up the incline. Suddenly, air whooshed over them. Turning and stumbling backward, Linc watched as the ebony shale buried the machine. Silence settled with the dust around them.

Then, another roar… Every inch of ground and air around them trembled. There was no time to think. Ryan and Mike backpedaled from where a new slide of shale closed off the opening ahead of them.

Then silence. Heavy silence, almost too quiet to be real, pressed on his ears. Nothing broke it for a long minute until the sound of their rasping breaths whispered through the air.

The only light came from the lamps on each hard hat. Beams of white light bounced back at them from the black dust in the air. Linc tried not to think how much of that crap was coating the inside of his lungs as he fought to breathe.

Linc moved first, his training kicking in. "I'll take this side." He checked the gas meter in his pack. No danger levels—yet. He kept the meter close.

Removing the lamp from his hard hat, he used it like a flashlight. Ryan and Mike did the same. Gabe and Zach settled Casey on a level patch of ground, while Robert tried to activate the emergency radio from Casey's belt.

Each man quickly took a section of the cavern, ringing it with light, looking for any indication of a breach in the rock. Linc found nothing. When he rejoined the others, they all shook their heads.

Even Robert. "Radio's crushed. I can't fix it." He tossed the broken pieces onto the ground and cursed.

They were well and truly trapped.

The one encouraging thing was that there had been no more rumbles. Obviously, they'd hit something with the blade, but what? With luck, only this chamber was affected. Little good that did them. Linc knew from the schematics of the mine that at least fifty feet of solid rock separated them from any hope of escape.

Gabe hunkered down next to Casey. They all watched his light illuminate Casey's leg. The steel-toed boots he wore had protected his foot, but his calf and knee had been severely chewed up by the tread of the machine. Blood soaked both his leg and the ground around him.

Gabe loosened Casey's belt and carefully slipped it off. "I can't stop the bleeding with just pressure." In minutes, he'd wrapped the man's leg in one of the thick flannel shirts he'd worn and tightened the belt around his upper thigh. "I trained as an EMT years back. I hoped I'd never need it," Gabe said, pain in his voice. "We'll have to watch him close."

At least Casey wasn't going to bleed to death in front of them. Not yet anyway.

The miners settled back, regrouping, their thoughts probably as disjointed as Linc's.

Trapped. They were trapped.

Linc fought the panic that clawed at his chest and knew it was probably a losing battle. He closed his eyes, picturing the house he had left only a few hours before. Home. He just wanted to go home.

He didn't dare picture Julia's face. That would be his undoing.

CHAPTER THREE

JULIA REACHED OVER and turned on the car's radio. Usually, after a day with her students, she appreciated the solace of silence. Now she needed something to drown out her thoughts.

Tomorrow would be her and Linc's seventh anniversary. Would he even remember? Or care? She shook her head. Linc might forget, but at one time he had cared. A lot. She blinked away the sting in her eyes. She refused to let him hurt her anymore.

Focusing on the road, Julia took in the sights of the small town she'd called home for just over a year. It seemed as though their problems had all started when they'd moved here, but she realized it wasn't the town's fault. It was actually a nice little place.

Parilton stood nestled between two hills the locals generously referred to as mountains. To Julia, who had spent her youth going skiing in the Rocky Mountains on vacations, they appeared small.

Still, they were familiar, and with spring in full bloom, the entire valley was green and colorful with blossoms.

The sight helped lift her mood as she hurried across

town. She wanted to get to the house before Linc—her soon-to-be-ex-husband, she reminded herself—got home from work. She hoped to get all of her things out without facing him.

Why did that thought sit so uncomfortably in her chest? She wasn't up to another fight. The last one still hurt, but not to see him?

She drove through the narrow streets of the town. Past the bank—the one and only bank—past the hardware store, past the Clever Curl Salon. One of the two stoplights in town turned red just as she reached it. The car stopped, but her thoughts kept going.

Did she and Linc even have anything left to save? Since they'd moved here, everything had changed. Without warning, the distant memory of Linc making love to her filled her mind. She closed her eyes, letting the image of his beautiful body soak into her internal vision. She could almost feel him, smell his clean scent, taste his warm breath…

"Oh, my." Her eyes flew open and she cranked the air conditioning. It had been too long since they'd had make-up sex. But when they had…

Memories and pain made her step a bit too hastily on the accelerator when the light changed. She refused to think about that anymore. It hurt too much.

She passed the grocery store and slowed. Parilton wasn't big enough for more than one, and it didn't even merit a national chain. But the local grocer carried nearly everything anybody needed. The bare cupboards of her newly rented apartment came too easily to mind.

The empty parking spot in front was like an invitation.

She pulled into it and sat staring through the grimy windshield. She'd never felt so alone.

Minutes later, she was rushing through the aisles, filling the basket with all the staples to make meals for one and trying to outrun her thoughts. It wasn't much, she realized as she looked at the pathetic pile of goods in the basket. Only one person stood in the checkout line. She could get out of here quickly.

The older woman checking groceries smiled at her. Rita Sinclair was Ryan's mother.

Julia's anger at Linc resurfaced. Why couldn't his inspection report mention the number of kids like Ryan working the mine—kids who should be in school? Her anger was at the system, but he hadn't helped at the meeting the other night. When had he lost faith in her?

"Hi, Julia." Rita smiled as she ran the items across the beeping scanner.

"Hello, Rita. How's everyone?"

"Fine." Rita examined the contents of Julia's basket, left eyebrow rising. "That's everything?"

Julia still didn't like the familiarity of small-town life. That's why she often drove into Pittsburgh to do her shopping. "Yes," she hedged and Rita didn't make any more comments.

"That's $27.57."

Julia handed over two twenties, and, as Rita counted out her change, she curled her fingers gently around Julia's hand. Julia looked up and was surprised to see the sheen in Rita's eyes.

"I want to thank you for all you did to try to get Ryan to stay in school."

Julia stared at her in surprise. "I...I wasn't sure if you agreed."

"My husband didn't. He thinks what was good enough for him is good enough for his boys. I'd like better for them." Her voice broke on the last words.

"Me, too," Julia whispered. "I haven't given up."

Their eyes met and for a long moment neither spoke. Someone moved into the line, and Julia didn't bother looking to see who.

Rita transformed from a mom back into the efficient grocery clerk and handed Julia her receipt. "You have a nice day."

"You, too."

Rita's words haunted her all the way to the car. That was what she'd tried to convey to Linc, though not very well. Why couldn't he understand? Why couldn't any of them understand? She quickly put the groceries in the car, avoiding the pain that went along with those thoughts.

She needed to move on, and today was the day for that to begin.

She drove too fast through town. She wanted this over and done with. Pulling into the drive, Julia sat there staring at the little house they'd bought within weeks of moving here.

She'd fallen in love with it the instant she'd seen it. She hated that Linc was the one still here, but she'd been the one to walk out. She'd left it and him behind.

The shades were all drawn, which grated on her

nerves and gave the house a dejected look. She loved the shades open, loved watching the sunshine pour in on the old wood floors. She tore her gaze away and took in the entire place.

It looked sad and neglected. This was ridiculous. She'd only been gone six days.

She shoved the car door open and walked up to the porch. She hesitated when she pushed the key into the lock then mentally berated herself. This was still her house, damn it. She stepped inside and decided maybe it wasn't.

The air was stale and warm. She longed to open the windows to let the rooms breathe, but she wasn't planning to be here that long. She turned to finish her packing but stopped in the bedroom doorway.

Frowning, she stepped inside, over two pairs of Linc's shoes. Her heart sank. She'd worked so hard to make this a room for relaxation, for privacy, for romance.

And now look at it.

"Linc, you idiot," she whispered. "I can't believe this."

The bed wasn't made, and as she sat down on the rumpled down comforter, she realized the same sheets were still on the bed as when she'd left. A pile of clothes grew in the corner by the rocker. Three beer bottles sat on the nightstand on his side of the bed.

What was wrong with him? He wasn't the neatest person in the world, but he'd never been a slob.

And alcohol? He wasn't one to drink…not in bed… not unless… Suddenly a memory of their honeymoon and a bottle of cheap champagne surfaced. *No.*

Julia shot to her feet. This was *not* her problem any-more. Determined to get this over and done with, she went to the closet and yanked out the first load of hang-ers. They grew heavy as she lugged them to the car. She'd piled several empty boxes in the back of the car, and she pulled them out to make room for the rest of her clothes.

She took the boxes to the bedroom and tossed her sweaters inside. She'd just opened her lingerie drawer, where a Pandora's box of emotions waited for her, when she heard the distant ringing of the phone. She ignored it, staring at the full drawer. Each silky garment held a memory of at least one night…

She didn't want to do this. It felt as though she was ripping her entire life to shreds with her bare hands. "Damn you, Linc." She grabbed a handful of silk and threw it into the box. She didn't care if the lingerie wrinkled. She'd never wear it again, but she wasn't leav-ing it behind, either. "Damn you. Damn you. Damn you." She crammed handfuls into the box in time with her words.

The phone started ringing again. Why wasn't the answering machine picking up? She stood and stalked to the kitchen where the only phone hung on the wall.

After seeing the bedroom, she'd thought Linc would've trashed this room, as well. But he hadn't. It was exactly as she'd left it.

Had he even come in here? Walking around the counter, she realized that, yes, he had been here. The trash can overflowed with takeout containers and paper plates. And the remnants of the answering machine that had been smashed to pieces.

Curious, she opened the pantry. The same three boxes of cereal she'd left sat there, untouched. How about the fridge? She hesitated to open it, knowing she'd left half a gallon of milk.

She breathed a sigh of relief. The milk was gone, but all that sat on the shelves was a six-pack of beer and a dozen sodas. She grabbed a cola, enjoying the feel of the cool metal against her hand.

"Serves him right if he starves to death," she mumbled and closed the fridge. Linc was a grown man. She refused to worry about him—he certainly didn't worry about her. The sound of the phone ringing yet again startled her, and she turned to glare at it. She didn't live here anymore, so why should she answer?

What if it was Linc? He knew she was going to be here today. Didn't she want to talk to him?

It kept ringing, loud in the quiet house. *Might as well get this over with.* "Hello," she snapped.

"Mrs. Holmes?" A stranger's deep voice came through the line.

Probably a salesman. How did they know to time this stuff? "Yes?" She sighed, not wanting to be rude, but not wanting to talk, either. Maybe she'd sign Linc up for whatever they were selling. Magazines? A burial plot? She knew she was being petty, but anger was easier to deal with than the hurt.

"This is David Hutchinson with the State Police. There's been an accident at the Winding Trail Mine." His voice was too distant, too rehearsed, as if he'd already said this a dozen times. "The family staging area is at the high-school gym."

Everything inside Julia drained away. For an instant the world tilted sideways just a bit. She closed her eyes, shutting away her emotions. *No. No.* She heard a thud, then a metallic rolling sound in the distance as she dropped the unopened soda.

This wasn't possible.

They'd been through the disaster drills dozens of times. Just because she received a call didn't mean a thing. Everyone was called and until all the families were there, no one would know who was getting the bad news.

Company policy. Long-standing practice. Damned frightening reality.

She fought not to panic but knew the turmoil in her stomach was just that. She didn't remember hanging up the phone, but it was back in its normal place. Had the man even really called? Was this a dream? *Please wake me up.*

What if…? Her knees nearly buckled. Where was Linc? She stared at the kitchen. What had she been doing?

Through the pounding in her ears, she heard the crunch of tires on the drive. Julia looked out the window, hoping, praying that it was Linc's truck. She'd give him an earful for scaring her half to death.

No such luck. A patrol car pulled in behind her sedan. She watched as the two officers climbed out. They didn't even have to knock as she met them at the door.

"Hello, Julia."

"Hello, Hank." Their next-door neighbor was a good man, always waving and smiling. He and Linc often stood out back and talked about guy stuff—fishing, football and lawn-mower parts. The other officer looked familiar, but for the life of her she couldn't think of a name.

"I thought you might need a ride," Hank said. He didn't bother to explain. Her face probably told him more than even she knew she was thinking and feeling.

"I think I can drive." She doubted she'd even remember how to start the engine.

"I'll drive your car so you've got wheels to come back home when you need to." Hank nodded toward the other officer. "Dennis will follow in the squad car."

She nodded. On autopilot, she grabbed her purse and keys and closed the door. Settled in the passenger seat, she looked back at the house as Hank climbed behind the wheel of her half-loaded car. It looked the same as it had just a few minutes ago—just as it had when she'd driven away on Friday, leaving Linc and it behind—and yet everything was different.

She was different. Numbness took over. Numb was good.

Thursday Afternoon, Two Hours Underground

THE ONLY PERSON WHO SEEMED capable of movement was the kid. Ryan moved about, trying to help Casey settle more comfortably on the hard stone floor.

The rest of them sat silently, watching the dust motes dance in the beam of their lights.

Linc had been through dozens of disaster drills. As a mine inspector, he'd set up several, coordinating with all the necessary teams: Search and Rescue, Fire, Emergency Medical Services and even Navy Dive teams for mine flooding. He'd coordinated, instructed, observed and participated. He knew the risks of mine work.

But he'd never faced the real thing. He swallowed the lump of panic in his throat.

"What the hell happened?" Linc growled softly, afraid that any noise would bring the rest of the roof down on their heads.

Gabe answered first. "That's a good question."

"We hit something too hard to be normal." Robert spoke from the darkness. He'd turned his lamp off. "Sounded like a rock bolt to me, but it should have been another six feet to the left. And we weren't cuttin' that high."

"Look." Gabe pulled the guide map he'd picked up in his assignment box before the shift. He handed the frequently folded and now grubby map over to Linc.

Pulling the light off his hard hat, Linc studied it. Taken from a larger map, probably one the owners had purchased from the Bureau of Land Management, it was worn in several places. He noted the marks that indicated the rock bolts' position. The eight-foot-long bolts that were drilled into the rock to stabilize the roof were normally six feet apart.

He stood and paced off the perimeter. Then he figured the distance again. Gabe watched him carefully. He could feel the older man's gaze drilling into his back.

He knew that Gabe was the kind of man who'd take

the responsibility for whatever went wrong. But Linc's gut was telling him this wasn't the crew's fault.

"Gabe, look here," he said.

The crew chief's footsteps came up behind him. "What?"

"See this outcropping?" Linc pointed to the rock and then the map. "There's supposed to be two rock bolts between here and there." He pointed to another mark on the map.

"Yeah. We must have cut the one." Gabe jabbed the map with a grubby finger.

"No. We were at least six feet from there, like Robert said. And even if we cut that one—where's the second?"

They looked at each other. Gabe paced off a few more feet, stopping at the edge of the slide. He shone his light up and stared as Linc watched his eyes widen. Linc moved over to stand beside Gabe and looked up.

There in the circle of the lamplight was a dark hole. Where the ceiling bolt was supposed to be was nothing. No sign of any bolt. Anywhere.

The hair on the back of Linc's neck tingled. All the reasons he'd become a mine inspector came clearly to mind.

Acts of God or Mother Nature were one thing.

The hand of man was something altogether different.

CHAPTER FOUR

Thursday Afternoon, 4:30 p.m.

HANK DROPPED JULIA OFF at the family staging area at the high school. It was in the same gym where she'd just attended a pep rally.

She walked through the familiar doors and looked around. The bleachers were full, but the laughing, smiling high-school students had been replaced by the sad, worried faces of miners' families. Some of those same kids were here again, their smiles erased by fear.

The only sounds in the room were those of restless bodies, tense whispers and her footsteps as she crossed to the bleachers. Her heels were entirely too loud on the polished wood floor.

She settled on the end of a bench, a bit away from the crowd, and wrapped her arms around her waist. She needed to hold herself together.

No one had said a thing yet. There was no word as to exactly who was in the trapped crew. This wasn't one of those times where no news was good news.

Voices came from everywhere around her. Soft, hushed voices. Wobbly, worried voices. Broken, pained voices. As a teacher, Julia had learned to eavesdrop in order to stay a step ahead of her students. Turning that skill off now was impossible. The fear and apprehension were alive and dark here in the room with her.

Sitting on the edge of the hard seat, she tried to hang on to her sanity. It wasn't easy. She looked around and the anguish she saw in the other faces cut through her. She couldn't look at them. It hurt too much to see their pain.

What was she doing here? she asked herself. She'd left him, ended their life together. She didn't owe Linc anything.

With a quick glance around the crowd, Julia felt a trace of guilt. No one knew the truth about their marriage because they hadn't told anyone. If she hadn't come, what would they think of her? Of Linc?

If he was dead—

She shuddered. *Linc.* She repeated his name in her head, praying that somehow that could make him appear before her. For the first time in days, she closed her eyes and pictured his face. Not the face that had been lined with anger and red with rage as he argued with her. Not the face of the man who silently drank his coffee each morning before work and barely spoke to her. Not the face of the man who strode from the house the other night.

She saw the boy she'd had a crush on all through high school. The boy she'd stayed up late with cramming for finals in college. The man whose face shone in completion as he made love to her.

The angry things she'd said that last evening at the house echoed around her. She closed her eyes. She didn't mean them. She swore she didn't. Pain clogged her throat and she fought the urge to curl in on herself.

"Ms. Holmes?" a young voice said beside her.

Julia's eyes flew open and she looked down to see one of her former students, Miranda Olsen, standing beside her on the bleacher below. The girl had to be six now. Her dark auburn curls fell from Hello Kitty ponytail holders on each side of her head. She'd grown up since she'd left Julia's kindergarten class last year.

"Hello, Miranda." The teacher in her stepped forward and the scared-to-death wife slunk back into the dark corners of Julia's mind. "It's nice to see you. How are you?"

"I'm in first grade now." She confirmed Julia's earlier thoughts. "I'm here with Mama. Daddy's in the mine."

Julia felt the bile rise in her throat. The idea of this child suddenly being fatherless was too much. Just too much. "I'm sorry."

"Why are you here?" The little girl tilted her head sideways.

"My…my husband…" Children didn't know a thing about legal separations and divorces. They shouldn't anyway. "My husband is down in the mine."

Miranda reached out a pudgy hand and patted Julia's fists. "It'll be okay, Ms. Holmes. My daddy will take care of him. He takes care of all of us."

"Oh, honey," Julia resisted the urge to pull the girl into her arms and hug her tight, to absorb some of that naive confidence. She was afraid that if she held her, she might not be able ever to let go.

"Miranda?" A woman's voice came from behind Julia. "Come back up here."

Julia didn't have to turn around to picture the woman's face. She remembered her from parent-teacher conferences.

"But, Mama, it's Ms. Holmes. She's really sad. I need to help her."

Even a six-year-old recognized her pain. Mortified, Julia sat up straighter. "Thank you, Miranda." She covered the tiny hand with her own. "You have helped me. I feel much better now," she lied. She couldn't let the girl take on that responsibility. She knew she'd succeeded when Miranda smiled.

"Okay." Miranda leaned closer, and as only a child could do, she put her hand against her mouth as if to whisper a secret. "It's okay to be scared. Daddy said he's scared sometimes, too."

The girl's image swam behind the tears that flooded Julia's eyes. The silence grew and Julia reached out to give a gentle tug to one of her ponytails and urged her to mind her mother.

Please let him be okay. Let them all be okay.

Miranda climbed back up on the seat beside her mother, and Julia didn't dare look around at her or at the rest of the crowd. Instead, she stared at the gym floor, thinking of another floor, another high school, another time.

She and Linc had known each other all their lives. At least they'd known *of* each other. In first grade, the same age Miranda was now, they'd both been in Mrs. Schwartz's class at Preston Elementary school, just outside Philadelphia. Linc had been a wild hellion at that age. He'd gotten his kicks from hiding things, like frogs and bugs, in the girls' desks or lunch boxes.

She almost let herself smile at the memory of how many times he'd been sent to the principal's office. That hadn't stopped him, of course. He just became more creative. She'd sworn she hated him.

Until high school.

Suddenly he'd seemed different. Taller. Less disruptive. Handsome. She hadn't understood then what she'd felt for him. Desires, some good, some bad—and some she thought were supposed to be bad—kept up a constant battle within her.

He'd been withdrawn their junior year, and she knew it had to do with his father's death. Linc had had to face the reality that sometimes people were lost deep in the mines. This was his worst fear.

She might be angry with him, and their marriage might be a mess, but she didn't wish him harm or…

Please, God. Don't let him die alone in the dark.

Thursday Afternoon, Two Hours Forty-Five Minutes Underground

"WE GOT WALLS TO BUILD, boys." Gabe's words shattered Linc's thoughts. Everyone except Casey stood.

The crew chief was right, work would keep their hands and anxious minds busy. Besides, building walls was an old miners' survival strategy. After a cave-in, walls helped stabilize the existing roof supports and, by barricading themselves into a small area, the miners could, they hoped, conserve their body heat and block out any toxic gasses.

"I'll see if I can get the battices. That end of the work site's still clear." Robert left to retrieve the canvas cloth stored near the work site for just this reason.

Gabe nodded. "Ryan, head over to the machines and see if you can find any of those bottles of distilled water." Ryan turned to leave. "But be careful. Don't move anything to get them."

"Yes, sir." Ryan vanished into the darkness, nothing but a bobbing light to indicate his existence.

"Zach, Mike, when Robert gets back, help him get that canvas up." He paced off space. "Here to here."

"Got it," Mike assured him. Zach nodded.

"I can help." Linc hated having to remind anyone of his existence. Gabe looked hard at him; Linc knew he wasn't really a part of this team.

"All I want you to do is keep an eagle eye on that meter. Check everyone's tanks. Regularly."

Gabe hadn't forgotten him, after all. He'd assigned each man the job he could do best. A little of Linc's anxiety eased as his faith in Gabe rose.

Robert returned, Ryan close on his heels. The three bottles of water were a welcome sight.

"Look what else I found." Ryan held up a battered lunch pail.

"I told you not to move anything." It was obvious the pail had been buried under something.

"It wasn't under anything but a couple of rocks."

"All right. Let's get this done." Already, Gabe's voice was raspy. The thick air was affecting them all. They had to get the barrier up before they lost all their strength. As it was, the task took more effort than normal.

The space they sectioned off was small and close, but it was the best hope they had of surviving until the rescue teams came for them.

They struggled with the large canvas, stumbling a couple of times because of the difficulty breathing. Twice, Zach left and had to crouch down to catch his breath. Finally, the large sheet in place, they all settled down to regain their strength.

Linc felt the exhaustion and lethargy creep over him. He stared at the white canvas wall—what he could see of it in the dim light, anyway. Somehow, it seemed they were admitting defeat by putting it up, but it was the only thing they had. Now all they could do was wait and try to stay alive.

Leaning back against the cold, rough wall, Linc closed his eyes. Were these men's faces and that damned wall of fabric the last things he'd ever see? Had this been what his father had experienced?

Memories of that long-ago day surfaced. His father's last day.

The news had come that there had been a cave-in. The families all gathered aboveground, just as they probably were doing right now. Absently, Linc looked up, as if he could somehow see through the mountain of rock. Had they gotten in touch with Julia? Would she even come?

Did she even know he was alive? Did anyone believe they'd survived? Were they going to dig for them, or had everyone given up and left the mine to be their tomb?

Questions and images flew at him from everywhere inside his head.

He remembered his mother's collapse that day. She'd never been the same after that. The broken, wailing woman had looked and sounded nothing like the mother he'd known for sixteen years.

As she'd crumbled, he'd put his arms around her, tried to comfort her, tried to absorb her tears into his young embrace. He'd tried but never quite succeeded.

He thought about Julia and couldn't imagine her crumbling like that, but he hadn't expected it of his mother, either. Did Julia even still care enough to hurt for him? Panic shot through him. At least his mother had had him and his brother to comfort her.

Julia had no one.

And that was his fault. He'd moved her away from her parents. Away from her friends to a strange and—according to her—inhospitable town. He'd done worse than his own father. He'd left her totally alone.

Guilt clawed in his chest as if some creature that had possessed him for years now fought to dig its way out.

She wanted children. Desperately. He'd been the one who hadn't really cared. He'd rarely considered having kids of his own, swearing he wouldn't leave them as his father had left him. But he'd always tried to give Julia everything he could.

A sound, a sob, broke from his throat. He smothered it with a groan and rose to his feet. He smacked his shoulder on the rock wall but suffered the pain in silence, accepting the punishment for his own selfish stupidity.

"What are they doing up top?" Ryan's voice shook. Linc realized all of their emotions were kicking in without any physical activity to distract them.

"They'll drill an air shaft first," Gabe whispered from the far corner as if fighting his own fears.

"Yeah," Linc agreed, hoping. "Fresh air. Man, won't that be nice?" Perhaps he'd get another chance. Perhaps, he prayed, not even sure what he was praying for, but knowing it couldn't hurt.

Wouldn't that surprise Julia? Him. Praying. He shook his head and smiled. The movement pulled the tight skin of his dry lips and the twinge of pain reminded him they all needed water.

"Where are those water jugs?" he asked. The water was kept down here for the machines but came in handy in times like this.

"Over by Casey," Ryan answered.

Linc found them easily. He opened one and took a deep swallow, then passed it to Ryan. "Take some. We need to stay hydrated." Ryan nodded and drank. Everyone followed suit and they even managed to get some down Casey's throat.

Linc sank back down to his spot on the ground. He'd be damned if he was giving up.

Julia might be up there. She might not, but he was going to do everything in his power to get back to her so they could at least fight it out face-to-face.

He had to hold on to that anger. It might be all he had.

Thursday Afternoon, 5:00 p.m.

THE STEEL DOORS AT THE END of the gym burst open, sending Julia's heart into her throat. Men covered in soot, their clothes grimy with it, flooded into the gym.

Everyone in the bleachers stood. Looking, seeking the man they'd spent the past few hours agonizing over.

Fervently, Julia searched. Too tall. Too short. Too heavy. While all the men looked alike in their dirty coveralls and blackened faces, none of them remotely resembled Linc.

Her stomach tensed and her chest burned as she held her breath. Tears flowed and men hugged women, children and each other. Slowly, the crowd thinned as families left. Surely she'd find him soon. Or he'd find her.

Lord knew she longed for that instant when she'd see him, recognize him. Would he hug her tightly? She wouldn't even care if the mine soot ruined her clothes. Or would he simply look at her with that painful silence and turn away as he had so many times lately?

She didn't care right now. She just wanted him here, safe. She couldn't be his wife anymore, but she didn't want him hurt, either.

Still, he didn't appear.

The fluorescent lights overhead dimmed. The noise of the crowd faded.

He wasn't coming. She knew it. Knew deep down inside that he was with that ill-fated crew.

"Oh, God," she whispered and felt the bench come

up to meet her. She wanted to bury her face in her hands and weep but didn't dare, just in case she missed him.

"Daddy!" Miranda's high-pitched squeal shattered the din. Miranda's father, grungy and filthy, swept her up in his arms. She giggled despite the smudge of black he left on her cheek where he kissed her.

"Daddy, did you help Ms. Holmes's husband?"

He frowned in confusion.

"Oh, sweetie." Julia stood again and reached out to stop the girl's words before they could rush out, but Miranda wasn't having any of that.

"Your husband?" Mr. Olsen—Julia couldn't remember his first name at the moment—looked at her in confusion, then as recognition dawned, he frowned. "Is he down there?"

She couldn't speak. All she could manage was a shrug. She longed for the days when a daddy could fix all the world's problems.

"We're going back down, ma'am."

"Ben, no." His wife held tight to his hand, snuggled up against his side and laid her head on his shoulder.

"You know that's how we do it," he whispered.

Tears in her eyes, the woman nodded. "I know."

Julia looked at the small family, her longing so thick it nearly stopped her heart from beating. She wanted a family of her own, but right now she was far away from having anything close to that.

"Holmes, right? He's the inspector?" Ben's voice broke into her thoughts. "He's a good guy. Not like some inspectors. He's fair. We'll get him out."

She believed him. Linc would do the exact same

thing. That look of determination in Ben's eyes was identical to the one she saw so often on Linc's face.

How had she missed that?

She swallowed hard and sat back down before she fell over. She watched the Olsen family leave. Miranda and her mother turned toward home, comfortable in the knowledge their husband and father was safe. Ben turned back to the mine to help find the others. Find Linc.

Just before the door closed, Julia saw Ben pull his wife close and kiss her long and deep.

She wanted to tear her gaze away, but she couldn't. An ache grew in her throat and she tried to remember the last time she'd been kissed like that.

She couldn't remember.

What was wrong with her that she couldn't stay in love with her husband? The thought hit her hard. Did she even love Linc anymore? She missed being held and loved and the company. She hated being alone. But did she actually miss *him?*

She didn't miss the anger and the frustration that came with waking up each morning.

"Mrs. Holmes?" A neatly dressed young woman touched Julia's shoulder, interrupting her thoughts. "Hello," the woman said softly, not waiting for Julia to respond, as if she feared Julia might break from the sound of her voice. "I'm Elizabeth Wilson."

Julia stared at her.

Elizabeth must have realized Julia wasn't going to, or couldn't, speak. "I'm a counselor. I thought maybe you'd like some company." Without waiting for an invitation, the woman sat down beside Julia.

That's when Julia's hope slipped. Linc was trapped underground. Perhaps even—she nearly retched at the thought—perhaps even dead.

She looked around at the suddenly surreal world. Few families remained. Those still seated had bleak, pained looks on their faces. She recognized Rita, Ryan's mother, the woman who'd spoken to her only a few hours ago at the grocery store. She saw Rita's husband and daughter-in-law, Rachel.

Julia's heart ached. Rachel Sinclair's presence meant that both brothers were down there with Linc.

She saw Shirley Wise and her heart rate increased a bit with hope. It felt a bit better knowing Gabe was with him. It was common knowledge around town that Gabe Wise was one of the most experienced miners. If anyone knew that mine, he did.

She didn't recognize the others but she did recognize their pain, their anguish.

Suddenly, just as before, the doors slammed open. No miners entered this time.

A group of men wearing suits came in and closed the doors behind them. She recognized the mine superintendent and a couple of other management types, but most of the frowning men were strangers to her. An uncomfortable feeling settled in her chest, and she knew she'd be getting to know them all too well.

Never before had she felt so trapped. She rebelled against it and stood. She wanted to leave, to run away, but knew she wouldn't. Couldn't leave without knowing what had happened.

"Who are they?" she asked the woman beside her, the counselor whose name she'd already forgotten.

The woman didn't answer. She simply stood and put her arm around Julia's shoulders.

Julia jerked away. "Don't touch me. Don't patronize me. Just answer me. Is my husband dead?"

CHAPTER FIVE

Thursday Afternoon, Three and a Half Hours Underground

LINC FELT RATHER THAN SAW Ryan scoot down beside him.

"What will they do after the vent shaft is done? How are they gonna get us out through that pile?" The kid tilted his head toward the caved-in exit.

"I'm not sure. There's a couple of options." At least he hoped so. "They'll lower a camera first, then a listening device and something to test the air. Don't worry. They *are* trying to find us." He didn't add that the rescue teams were probably still trying to figure out if they were even alive. "Hopefully, they'll pump in the fresh air first."

Ryan coughed as if on cue to show how bad the air had become. "That'd be good." He didn't say anything else but didn't move away, either.

"Relax. Breathe slow," Linc prompted. They all carried a self-contained breathing apparatus as part of their emergency kits. It gave them a limited amount of good air and no one wanted to waste it. So far, Linc's meter had been clear of any readings for toxic gas, but the dust made it difficult to take a clean breath. He kept a close eye on the gauge.

Linc waited until Ryan had relaxed before he spoke again. "Something on your mind?"

"Uh, yeah. I been thinking. About stuff. 'Bout school. Mrs. Holmes is gonna be mighty pissed at us, huh?"

Linc almost laughed. He was pretty sure that was how Julia felt about him most of the time. His gut tightened as he thought about the hell the families must be going through. Part of him hoped Julia wasn't up there, that she'd managed to stay untouched by this. The selfish part of him prayed she was waiting for him. "Why do you say that?" He focused on Ryan instead.

"She was so mad when I told her I was quitting school."

"Yeah, I know. Why exactly did you quit?"

"You aren't going to get on my case, too, are you?"

"No. Just curious." He was more than curious, but he knew better than to push. Ryan was the only one talking at the moment and Linc didn't want to lose this connection, no matter how tenuous it might be, to Julia.

In the dim light, Linc thought he saw the boy shrug. "I was having a tough time."

"Like how? Kids picking on you?"

"No!" Ryan looked over at Linc as if he might clam up. His denial was a bit too vehement, but Linc let it pass.

He waited for Ryan to continue.

"Math was kicking my butt. Mrs. Holmes kept trying to convince me I could do it. Said I just needed help, but that didn't work too well."

Something in the young miner's voice told Linc that

the attempt had caused more problems than it solved. He chuckled. "She ought to know."

"What do you mean?"

"She won't like me telling you." He almost didn't, but realized he wanted to talk about her. "She hated math in school. Flunked it twice in college."

He should be thankful for Julia's lack of math skills. Even when she kept her distance from him, it provided an excuse for her to ask him for help, though he honestly believed she could do it if she had more faith in her abilities. Too many abysmal failures, though, had left a deep mark.

"She said someone helped her in school."

"Yeah. I did." Linc smiled and leaned his head back against the hard rock. God, it felt good to remember and leave this dark, damp place for a moment.

He recalled the study sessions that had run late into the night. Her laughter. The frustration she'd expressed when she didn't understand. They'd grown close so quickly over those months. Was that why it had fallen apart just as quickly now?

"You've known her a long time?" The tone of Ryan's voice changed.

"Yeah. Since first grade. We went to school together."

"See!" Ryan leaned over toward his brother.

"Oh, here we go." Mike's voice came out of the darkness and Linc could almost hear the older brother roll his eyes.

"Shut up, Mike," Ryan said.

"What's going on?" Linc couldn't let Ryan's comment go without a response.

"Nothing," Ryan whispered.

"It doesn't sound like nothing. You got a question to ask? Do it." Something was bothering Ryan and he seemed to want to talk to Linc. Maybe it was because Linc was a stranger, or maybe because he was the only option at the moment. The others didn't seem too concerned with him.

"They all think I'm trouble." Ryan tilted his head to the group as a whole.

"Why?"

"'Cause I'm just a kid to them."

He *was* just a kid, but Linc realized there was no turning back now. Ryan had left his childhood behind the day he'd stepped through the mouth of this mine.

"When they reach us, getting out of here isn't going to be easy, you know," Linc offered. "We have to work together."

"*If* they reach us, you mean." Ryan's mood had deteriorated into seventeen-year-old attitude.

"No. When. Hey, look, you've got the edge on us all."

"What do you mean?"

Linc suddenly wished Julia was here to advise him. She knew how to deal with these kids. He hadn't a clue. He hadn't been seventeen in a very long time.

"What do you mean?" Ryan repeated, more of that attitude returning to coat his words.

"When the mine caved in at Sago, the lone survivor

was the youngest of the group," Linc said softly. Ryan didn't immediately reply.

"Why do you think that happened?"

"Partly because the others looked after him, thinking he was young and needed taking care of." Linc knew that wasn't going to thrill Ryan, even if it was true. "But also because he had more resilience and reserves. His body did better without air for a longer time."

Bodies shuffled and a soft snore came out of the darkness. Linc knew Ryan was thinking, he just wasn't sure what about.

"Linc?"

"Yeah,"

"When you were my age did you know what love was?"

Linc managed to swallow his initial shock. "Uh, yeah. I think so." Oh, good. He was messing this up, he was sure of it.

Looking back, though, he realized he wasn't lying. He had loved Julia, even back then, even before they'd gotten together in college. "Lord, you make me feel old, kid." He'd been in love with Julia for most of his adult life. Where had the time gone?

"You're not old. You're younger than my dad."

"Thanks. I think."

"Hey, that's not an insult. My dad's not horrible. He's just—"

"Be glad you've got him, kid. My dad died when I was sixteen. I never really got to tell him how I felt, and I certainly didn't get the chance to talk to him as an adult." Linc couldn't remember the last time he'd let himself think about his father, and he knew he'd never admitted that to anyone, including himself.

Something clattered in the darkness, startling them both. Ryan gave a nervous laugh and stood, as if looking for an escape from the conversation. "I'll go see what that was."

"Ryan, wait—" Linc leaned over to stop him but missed. "Don't go far," he called after him.

"Give up, man." Mike's voice came out of the dark. He'd obviously overheard their conversation. "Ry doesn't listen to anyone."

Linc laughed. "What seventeen-year-old does?"

"Fair enough." Mike chuckled, as well. It was good to hear the other man's voice without the overwhelming fear and concern in it. They all knew he was worried about his wife, Rachel. He'd spoken some about his parents, but mostly it had been about Rachel. Linc had met the shy woman a couple of times around town. She was pregnant with their first child, and Mike feared this would be too hard on her.

"You think he's too young to be in love?"

"He's only seventeen."

"How old are you, Mike?" Link had a vague idea but he wanted to hear the other man admit it.

"Twenty. Yeah, I know. Not much older, and I've been married almost two years. But I—"

"Feel older?"

"Yeah. Especially right now. When Rachel and I first got married, I thought we were on top of the world and could do anything we wanted." Linc remembered that feeling. Suddenly his mind filled with memories from his own wedding day. He couldn't remember a time in his life he'd been that nervous. That had scared him even more than being stuck down here did.

"But? What happened?"

"Life happened, man. We didn't exactly plan to have kids so soon. She's been going to college at night. She wants to be a nurse." Mike's pride exploded in the cavern. "She can't do that if I'm not there to help her." His pride vanished and fear took its place.

"Don't sell her short." Linc had always thought Julia couldn't survive without him. That damned male ego she was always accusing him of having. Okay, he was a guy. He knew that. He liked it. She was disgustingly right, though. She'd apparently done fine without him this week, as she hadn't come home, and that knowledge made him ache.

"When Rachel got pregnant she was actually mad at me for a week." Mike didn't sound like that bothered him too much. "But she got over it once she realized we were actually going to have a baby." His voice hitched.

"Until the morning sickness hit," Linc offered, then realized what he'd just confessed.

"Didn't know you had kids."

Linc swallowed the pain in his throat. "We...we don't. Julia miscarried. Five months along." They'd never discussed it with anyone outside of her family.

"Man, that's tough." Mike's voice came out way too soft. Linc had to change the topic or Mike was going to fall back into that depression he'd felt earlier.

"Do you know if it's a boy or a girl?" Linc asked, knowing that wasn't what he'd meant to say.

"Boy."

"That they're going to name after me," Ryan yelled from the other side of the cavern.

"Quit eavesdropping, brother."

"I can't help it." Ryan reappeared. "We're sorta stuck here together."

The brotherly banter made Linc smile. His own brother had left years ago, and he hadn't heard from him since. He missed it, he realized, thinking back on the years before his dad died. When they'd played together, teased each other, been a family.

Was that what Julia had wanted? The thought surprised him. He'd never bothered to ask her. And she'd never bothered to tell him. Or maybe he hadn't been listening.

He closed his eyes and, for the first time since the cave-in, let himself picture her as she had been back when he'd decided to act on his longtime attraction to her. He remembered it all so clearly. They'd been walking across campus that day. Tiny snowflakes had fallen from the leaden clouds and landed softly in her hair. He'd been fascinated by the sight. Even now his fingers itched to reach out and touch the thick copper-gold curls.

At that point, Julia hadn't seemed to even notice him and he'd been doing his best to ignore the attraction he felt for her.

Attraction. Hell, he'd been besotted with her. Did anyone even use that word anymore? His nights in college had been populated with hot dreams and cold showers. He remembered their first kiss. After a successful tutoring session, she'd launched herself at him in a thank-you hug that had quickly turned to something else. Something sweet and hot that had kept them close for long, endless minutes. He could still taste her and his body ached to hold her, touch her again.

Looking back, he realized that in all the years they'd been together, that day was probably the only time he'd truly believed in them. Was that part of the reason his marriage was in trouble now?

Julia was the daughter of a mine owner. Rich. Affluent. Linc was the son of a man who'd died in those mines. Poor. A nobody on life's radar. He opened his eyes and the reality of the cold mine came crashing back.

He'd known then that they weren't meant to be together, but he'd ignored his gut and married her anyway. He shivered, and not just from the cold, damp mine tunnel.

She'd finally walked out on him.

Time had proven him right.

Thursday Afternoon, 5:30p.m.

JULIA STARED AT THE FIVE MEN in suits who stood together at the front of the gym like bricks in an impenetrable wall. She immediately didn't like them and she liked them even less when they started to talk.

One man took a step forward. "I'm Martin Halston. I'm the CEO of the Winding Trail." His face flushed as if admitting that wasn't something he wanted to do. The bright red color swept up his pudgy neck and showed through his thinning salt-and-pepper hair. "I want you to know we're doing everything we can to figure out what happened."

Jack Sinclair stood. His face was red, too, but from anger not embarrassment. "My sons are down there," he shouted. "Right now I don't give a damn what happened. I want to know what you're going to do to get them out."

The silence stretched uncomfortably until finally another man stepped forward. What weren't they being told? Julia watched Halston stand back and take a deep breath.

"I'm Patrick Kelly, Director of the Mining Commission." This man seemed a bit more sure of himself. "That's why we're here. To fill you in." He pulled off his suit jacket and tugged at his tie before he spoke again. "There's been one face fall that we know about. There's debris, but we believe the men are beyond that. We've started drilling the first bore hole."

"Hell." Jack Sinclair threw his hands up in frustration. "You don't even know if they're alive, do you?"

"We're trying to find out. We hope so." Patrick scrubbed a hand over his face, then met Jack's eyes. "You wouldn't want me to lie, would you?" An awkward silence settled over them all.

"No."

Julia wasn't so sure. She wanted to hear that they were okay and would be home soon. *Lie to me. Lie to me.*

For several long minutes, she listened to the men argue. She understood Jack's pain. His two sons—his only children—were down there. She felt as if she were watching a bad dream through distorted glasses.

This *wasn't* real. It *couldn't* be real.

She didn't understand all the jargon they were throwing around, but she did understand that they were drilling down to try to locate the men. That wasn't going to be anytime soon, and forever stretched out in front of her. She knew from past incidents that this whole process—regardless of the outcome—could take hours, or even days.

She swallowed her anxiety and looked around at the people who shared her fear.

The Sinclair women sat behind Jack. Rita's arms were around her very pregnant daughter-in-law, Rachel. Shirley Wise sat to the side, her back ramrod straight as she glared at the men. For once, Julia and Shirley were on the same page.

Another woman sat on the front row of the bleachers. The blonde woman's face was buried in her folded arms.

Julia turned back to look at the young counselor who'd come to comfort her. Why had she come to her and not this heartbroken woman? Because of who her husband was? Julia fought a flare of anger. Neither she nor Linc wanted special treatment. She was in the same boat as everyone else here. Her loved one was trapped, too.

Her thoughts stopped. Loved one? She didn't love Linc anymore. Did she? Instead of an answer, a blank empty void threatened to suck her under. She had to escape her thoughts.

She stood and walked over to the distraught woman. Gently, Julia touched the woman's shoulder, trying not to startle her. The woman jumped anyway and stared at her. The pain in her eyes hit Julia like a semi barreling down I-99. She nearly took a step back from it.

"I didn't... I can't..." The woman took Julia's hand and squeezed it tight. Julia let her hold on, let herself hold on.

Julia settled beside the woman. Jack didn't look pleased with what Patrick was saying, but he sat next to his wife, who laid her head on his shoulder.

Julia closed her eyes and wished for a strong shoulder to lean on... The what-ifs that popped into her mind hurt too much. She forced herself to open her eyes and focus. She couldn't let herself feel right now.

"There's a press conference scheduled for six o'clock," Patrick said. Everyone turned to look at the large white-faced clock high up on the wall. Less than ten minutes from now. How had they been here for two hours already?

"Look." Patrick stood beside Jack now, his hand on the man's shoulder. "I don't have the answers for you. I wish I did. We've got crews and equipment headed this way from three states. We'll do everything humanly possible to get to our crew."

Julia realized they had to trust these men and that she had to put her faith in their knowledge, skill and determination. She didn't necessarily have to like them, but they needed this operation to succeed as much as everyone else in the room.

Jack stood and Patrick held up his hand as he spoke. "I *will* promise you one thing. I'll tell you everything I know as soon as I know it. And I'll tell you before I tell the press. Fair enough?"

Jack nodded once, then turned back to his wife. He suddenly looked defeated and years older than he had a moment ago.

Patrick's promise sounded sincere, but Julia couldn't help but wonder how he was going to keep it. She'd never felt more helpless and alone than she did surrounded by all these people.

The mine managers left the gym with what seemed like incredible speed. As they opened the metal doors, the flash of lights, the crush of microphones and reporters was surprising and intimidating.

Julia cringed. She couldn't deal with reporters. Not now. Her panic faded when the doors closed again.

Only one of the men remained. Patrick Kelly.

Julia stood, not letting go of the woman's hand. "What now?"

Patrick seemed relieved that someone else other than Jack had spoken. "We know from experience that you all need to be as close to the site as possible."

The shadow of past mining disasters fell across the group. They all knew the history, the successes and failures. Accurate communication was key, and Julia was relieved to hear that Patrick was aware of the risks.

"We're not going to try to run you in front of those reporters like others have done," Patrick said. "We've set up a tent near the command center. We'll get you all there as soon as the reporters are gone."

"That's not going to happen." Jack sighed in exasperation. "They're here for the duration. You know what the press is like with stuff like this."

"I don't know how else to get you through that crush." Patrick looked helpless and frustrated.

The thought of sitting here on the hard bleachers for any longer was too much. Julia wasn't sure she could do that without losing her mind.

"Isn't there another way out?" Shirley asked, rising from her seat.

"There is a back way." Julia blurted out the words as her mind clicked into gear. She'd caught two kids using it just last week.

"Back way?" Everyone looked at her expectantly.

She almost smiled. It felt good to be doing something, even something so simple.

"I just want out of here," the woman beside her whispered.

Rita spoke for the first time. "If you know how, show us."

"Come on." Julia helped the blonde woman to her feet and fumbled around in her pocket for her keys. The master key was something she seldom used, but she didn't think the principal would care if she used it now.

She led the group to the weight room just beyond the far doors. "There's a door behind that closet, left over from the renovation." She pointed it out and Patrick and

Jack moved the mats away. She slid her master key into the lock she'd had put on just last week.

"Hold on." Patrick pulled his cell phone out of his pocket and spoke into it. "Yeah. Bring it around to the back of the school." He cautiously pushed open the door and looked around. "And don't let anyone see you leave." After he hung up, he turned back to the families. "We've got a bus to take you up the hill."

"What about my car?" Shirley asked.

"We'll leave your cars here for now. It'll distract the press for a while at least."

The sound of a bus engine came through the opening in the door. "Let's go." Patrick led them outside. "If we hurry, maybe we can slip past before the press conference ends."

The sun hung low in the sky, and clouds blocked some of the fading twilight. A cool wind plucked at Julia's hair. She wondered where her jacket was. Had she even brought one?

Still holding the other woman's stiff hand, Julia led her across the grass to the yellow school bus. She would have preferred the physical activity of walking to the mine, but that wasn't an option at this point.

She felt better having remembered the door. She had to keep busy, had to take action. Doing kept her from thinking. She couldn't give in to her emotions. Not now. She had to be strong. Nothing else was an option.

As the bus turned the final corner out of the school parking lot, nearly everyone turned to look back. The press conference must have just ended, but the few reporters who had already stepped outside weren't quick enough to catch even the slow-moving bus. Moments later they drove through the gates of the mine and Julia breathed a sigh of relief. They'd escaped.

For now.

CHAPTER SIX

Thursday Evening, 6:30 p.m.

A HUGE WHITE TENT had been erected on a flat patch of ground behind the mine offices. It was one of those tents typically rented for happy events—weddings, bar mitzvahs or revival meetings.

As Julia climbed off the bus, she wondered if the canvas had soaked up enough good memories to counter the bad ones she was afraid lay ahead.

Stop that! She shook her head and tried to clear the gloomy thoughts. The quiet young woman at her side and the others shuffling behind her prompted her to keep moving.

Hank and Dennis, the other officer she'd met earlier, stood a few yards away at the gates to the compound, keeping the media out and the families in. She knew the mine didn't want any more bad press than necessary, which, for now, suited her just fine. There was no way she'd make it if she had to deal with reporters shoving microphones in her face.

The blonde woman suddenly spoke. "I'm Trish Hayes. My husband, Zach, is down there."

"Hi, Trish. I'm Julia." She tried to smile but found her facial muscles reluctant to cooperate.

"I know. Your husband's the inspector, isn't he?"

"Yeah."

"Maybe that's a good thing."

"Why?" Julia couldn't see anything good about any of this. She stumbled over a rock in the dirt path. Trish clutched her arm and kept her from falling on her face. They were definitely in this together.

"There are too many accidents. Maybe now we'll get some action from the mine owners and the government."

Julia sighed, doubting it. She hadn't been able to persuade Linc to include her concerns about kids working the mines in his report. He hadn't agreed with her. Was there any chance now that his report on this mine might make a difference?

What if he didn't come out of this even to file a report?

Before her panic could totally overwhelm her, she and Trish walked into the tent. She stepped into the sudden dimness, waiting while her eyes adjusted.

A row of cots had been set up in the back. Metal folding chairs and several long tables made up uneven rows. One table off to the side held a large coffeepot, cups and several covered dishes.

Bless the women of Parilton. They might not be able to dig for coal, but they sure could cook. Before this was over, the table would be laden with enough casseroles to feed an army.

And the rescue crews fit that bill. They'd wolf it down in between trips into the mine. Julia looked away from the food, away from the images it conjured of long hours spent not knowing.

Instead, she focused on the coffeepot. She craved a jolt of caffeine and led Trish to the table to fill a cup. The dark brew scalded her tongue and throat going down.

Perfect.

Voices came through the tent opening. Almost as one, she and Trish turned. Patrick led a small group inside. A big, burly man among them called out, "Trish. Where's Trish?"

Trish's arm left Julia's for the first time since that moment in the gym. A wave of loneliness swept over her as Trish moved away.

"Daddy," Trish cried and sped across the tent. The man enfolded her in his arms. She let loose and sobbed into the front of his flannel shirt.

Patrick lifted his hand. "Can I have your attention?" Everyone, including Trish, looked up hopefully. "I need you all to make a list of anyone who will be joining you here." Disappointment hung in the air as he handed out pieces of paper. "The police are going to keep everyone else out."

Shirley spoke up from the back of the group. "My daughter's going to be flying in from Georgia."

"Put her name on your list and we'll be sure to let her in. And if you talk to her, to anyone, tell them to have their ID handy."

Shirley stepped forward. "Has anyone contacted Mamie Hastings?"

"Who's she?" Patrick asked.

"Her son Robert's on Gabe's crew. He's down there,

I'm sure. I didn't see him come into the gym." She waited until Patrick nodded. "She lives over at Shady Pines Retirement Home in Hillsville."

"I doubt she knows," Patrick admitted.

"Well, someone better tell her."

"Do you think she's up to it?" Obviously, Patrick believed the elderly woman was too infirm.

Shirley chuckled. "You better send someone to go get her. She's liable to start heading this way with her walker if she sees it on the news."

"I'll check on it."

Julia figured Hank or Dennis would be headed over to Hillsville soon.

From her vantage point near the coffee station, Julia looked over the crowd. The families were grouped together and Patrick made the rounds. When he stopped in front of her, he hesitated.

"Are you here alone?"

She nodded, meeting his gaze, defying him to make an issue of it. He handed her a sheet of paper and a stubby pencil that had seen better days. The blank page blurred. She couldn't begin to think what to do with it. Instead, she folded it and shoved it into her pocket with the pencil.

Patrick moved away, but not before squeezing her shoulder.

Another man's voice startled her. "Are you Julia?" She looked up at the bear of a man who had hugged Trish.

"Y-yes."

He stuck out his hand. "Walt Robinson. I wanted to thank you for watchin' after my girl."

Julia nodded and slipped her hand into his. Her fingers were engulfed, and before she realized what he had in mind, he'd pulled her into a strong hug. She ached to turn into his embrace as Trish had, but instead she pulled back. She focused on the coffee he'd miraculously not spilled.

"Take care of her," she told him with a voice that seemed way too small and stepped away, letting the family have their privacy.

Over the next hour, several more people arrived and the melancholy reunion hugs were nearly incessant. Julia looked around, sipping yet another cup of coffee, a cup that became her focus, something to hold on to. People, strangers and neighbors, were everywhere. They pressed in close and the noise level rose to a dull roar.

She needed to get out of here. With her cup in hand, she stepped outside the quickly crowded tent.

She gulped in the cooling mountain air and felt her muscles relax a little. The scent of rain was heavy in the breeze, and as if summoned by her thoughts, drops started to fall around her. Still she didn't go back inside. She scooted up against the tent flap, out of the rain and away from the crowd.

Too many people made her nervous. If anyone touched her, or was too nice to her, she'd fall apart. She refused to let that happen.

Glancing at her watch, she realized three more hours had passed. How long had Linc been down there? Nearly five hours now. It seemed like five days. Five years. Forever.

Hold on. Please hold on.

Thursday Evening, Six and a Half Hours Underground

LINC STARED AT THE UNEVEN surface of the cavern's ceiling. It wasn't far away and even in the dim light, he made out the rough contour where the machine had ground the rock away from itself. The crew that would be searching for them had to go through that. Thinking about how much work needed to be done only added to his fatigue and worry.

He was tired. They all were. They were trying to conserve energy as best they could. Besides, what else did they have to do but wait?

Claustrophobia threatened and he bit it back. Panicking was not an option. Deep, slow breaths. He focused on listening to and slowing his own heart rate. He'd learned the techniques not long after his father's death, when the nightmares of being trapped first appeared. He'd conquered it then, he'd do it now.

"Gabe?" he called out into the void.

"Yeah?" The older man's voice was soft and seemed distant.

"What's the one thing you're going to do when we get out of here?"

Gabe chuckled. "Buy a burger, a big fat juicy one—to hell with my cholesterol."

Linc laughed.

"And you?"

Linc struggled to answer. "I don't know," he lied. He knew what he *wanted* to do, but making love to Julia was out of the question now. How long had it been? He had no clue and that didn't sit well with him. Where had the urgency gone that had filled those first years? He could clearly recall those days when they couldn't keep their hands off each other. Now he might never get the chance to touch her again. And not just because he was trapped here. She was probably completely moved out of the house by now.

Seven years of marriage gone. What was even left for him to go home to?

He closed his eyes against the oppressive dark. Maybe if he kept remembering everything, he'd somehow be stronger, more resistant to being erased by time or events. Maybe he'd live a little longer.

He glanced at his watch, the face glowing in the darkness with a press of a button. They'd been down here seven hours. He swallowed hard, fighting the panic that threatened to overwhelm him.

"Hey, Mike." Ryan called to his brother from where he sat next to Linc, breaking the cycle of Linc's thoughts.

"Yeah?" Mike didn't sound good.

"You think Dad's waiting up top for us?"

"Probably." Mike paused, then turned to look at his younger brother. "He knows, kid. He knows." Mike tried to reassure Ryan, but even to Linc's ears, he sounded scared.

Thursday Evening, 11:00 p.m.

JULIA HAD NEVER SEEN a night sky like this before. Floodlights brighter than sunshine shone over the valley.

Where the clouds had blocked the sun most of the day, those same clouds now reflected the light. The damp drizzle continued, reminding her just how at the mercy of the elements they all were.

True to their word, the mine owners had brought in crews of men and truckloads of equipment.

Also true to his word, Patrick came to the tent every half hour to keep the families informed. So far there had been precious little beyond the explanations of which teams were planning to do what.

Between meetings, the large tent had filled with more people. Julia could hardly stand the crowd.

She had learned more about Trish Hayes, who seemed to be the only person who realized Julia was even there. She told herself she preferred it that way. She discovered that Zach Hayes had worked this mine for nearly three years, and another one for five years before that. He and Trish didn't have any kids, either, which Trish considered a blessing at times like this.

Once again, Julia stood at her perch near the opening of the tent, mug in hand. The coffee had grown cold but she needed something solid to hold on to.

Just then, Hank's squad car pulled through the gates and stopped a few feet from the tent's entrance. He hurried around the car and pulled open the passenger door. He unfolded a metal walker and set it in front of the white-haired, elderly woman as she turned in the seat. Unfurling an umbrella with one hand, he helped her stand with the other. This must be Mamie Hastings. She wasn't as old as Julia had expected—probably in her mid-seventies—but obviously had trouble getting around on her own.

"Thank you, Hank." The woman smiled up at him. Julia recognized it as a courteous smile without any warmth. There was too much worry and pain in the old woman's eyes. She slowly stood and made her way toward the tent opening.

Hank looked over at Julia and waved his hand for her to join him and help. The look on his face told her he didn't know how to deal with this woman. Curiosity nudged her to his side. Julia walked along beside them, but Mamie did just fine.

"Shirley?" Hank called out as they stepped inside the tent. "Mamie's here."

Shirley rushed over and stepped in front of Julia, helping guide the old woman to one of the padded folding chairs.

Before she sat down, though, the woman gave Shirley a hug. "Thank you for sending for me. I hate my boy bein' down there."

"Well, we're all here together now." Shirley looked up at Julia. There wasn't any warmth in Shirley's gaze, either, but not just because she was worried.

Julia knew Shirley didn't like her. She'd never kept that a secret. Julia wasn't quite sure why, but she felt her enmity even now. Rather than introducing Julia to Mamie, Shirley helped the elderly woman get settled in a chair, and then went off to get her a drink.

"Hello." Julia stepped forward to introduce herself. "I'm Julia Holmes."

Again, Mamie flashed one of those too-polite smiles. "Yes, hello. The inspector's wife."

Once, just one time during all this, Julia wished someone would realize she was Julia, not "Mrs. Linc." Sighing, she put it down to the woman's age and the society in which she'd lived so much of her life. It didn't do any good letting it bother her. "Yes. I am."

"Nice to meet you, though I wish it were under better circumstances."

"Me, too."

Shirley returned and without acknowledging Julia, planted herself between Mamie and her. She patted Mamie's hand and filled her in on Patrick's last report. Mamie listened, slowly sipping her drink as her eyes grew more distant and her skin paled.

Julia stood back, feeling deliberately excluded and very much the outsider. She needed space, some fresh air, and, walking backward, she headed toward it. She grabbed one of the rain slickers that hung by the front entry and slipped it on. She needed more space than she could get in the doorway.

Outside, the air was cool and felt good after the heat in the tent from so many close bodies. She walked down the hill a short way, looking at the familiar outline of the mine and the new addition, the drilling rig atop the next hill. The skeletal frame had the appearance of a looming monster poised to attack.

Men scurried around, and she watched their head-lamps flash puddles of light across the uneven, damp ground. Just outside the mouth of the mine, another white tent had been erected. Inside two men huddled over a large table covered with papers and maps. Several miners nodded to her, but none stopped as they passed. She recognized their faces despite the grime that covered their features. Even the rain couldn't remove it all. Instead, the moisture sent dark streaks down onto their clothes.

She shivered and, despite the raincoat, cold slipped down her collar. At least she felt something.

Quick movements caught her eye, and she looked over in time to see Patrick hurrying across the grounds. Was he headed to the tent? Oh, God. What was happening? Had the crew been found? Were they… She didn't finish her thought.

As she turned, she saw the huddled mass of people beyond the property-line fence. The press. She knew they were here to cover a story. This was their job, no matter what the outcome.

Hank stood there, a silent sentry. His squad car sat behind him like an added reminder of the boundary. Still, Julia pulled up the hood of the borrowed, too-big raincoat to hide her face.

As she ran, she heard the crackle of the paper in her pocket. She hadn't put any names on it. Heck, she hadn't even thought to call anyone to let them know what was going on. It now occurred to her that her parents wouldn't appreciate being notified by CNN.

Linc's parents wouldn't need notification. The senior Mrs. Holmes had been gone two years now. She'd never have survived this. Julia closed her eyes and said a prayer to her mother-in-law for strength. She didn't even know how to contact his brother. She hadn't seen him since grade school. For him, CNN would have to do.

Moving on, she nearly slipped in the slick mud. Suddenly, a strobe light went off and Julia looked up. She instantly regretted it as half a dozen more flashes broke the darkness. The photographers had gotten a clear view of her face. She knew they probably wouldn't be able to identify her yet, but it was apparent from her lack of mining gear that she wasn't part of the rescue crews.

She wanted to curse and scream at them, but that was exactly what they wanted. They were here to get proof the families were falling apart, that they knew something the press didn't. Every one of them wanted to be the first reporter to get "the scoop."

Rather than give it to them, Julia pulled the coat closer and leisurely walked—as best she could through the muck and mud—to the tent. Keeping her eyes straight ahead, she hoped her expression remained neutral.

The gentle rat-a-tat of the rain on the canvas wasn't soothing. It grated on her nerves. Patrick wasn't anywhere in the tent that she could see. Maybe she'd been wrong. Where was he? Had she missed a report? The tent seemed no more tense than it had before. She relaxed a little.

Julia shoved her way through the crowd, looking for Patrick. She emerged on the other side of the tent to find nothing.

He wasn't anywhere to be found. Suddenly, even with all the bodies pressing close, all the voices floating around her, she felt very much alone. She didn't want to be alone anymore.

She should have called her parents already; despite the distance between them, they were her family. They might not be as loving as she'd like, but she knew she could count on them.

A row of phones sat on one of the tables for the families to use. Most everyone's cell batteries were dead and the heavy mountains made service spotty anyway.

Shirley Wise was using one phone, and Julia waited until she'd finished before walking toward the table. Her hand shook as she reached out to pick up the receiver.

She seldom spoke to her parents; their disapproval of Linc was so overwhelming. She hadn't even told them that she and Linc were separated. She couldn't think about that now. The whole world was falling apart. With trembling fingers, she punched in the familiar number.

"Hello."

"Mom? It's Julia."

"Oh, dear. We were just talking about you." Her mother's voice was so calm, so normal, so oddly comforting. "We saw on the late news where there's been some kind of mine disaster down there. Is it near you?"

She should have called sooner. Her stomach wound into knots as she forced her lips to form the words. "Linc's one of the men trapped." She was surprised at her mother's silence. She hadn't realized the woman had it in her.

"Is he…?"

"Is he what?" Julia couldn't let her mind go any further.

"Um, still alive?"

Julia actually appreciated her mother's hesitance. "We don't know, Mom."

For the first time since her marriage had failed, since this whole ordeal had begun, Julia's strength wavered. Once again she was a little girl frightened by nightmares. She wanted to feel her mother's arms and hear her reassurances—no matter how false—that everything would be fine. She had no idea what she was supposed to do. Everything seemed to crash in around her. The arguments of the past months. The pain of finally leaving Linc. The overwhelming fear that she might lose him permanently.

"Julia? Hon? Are you there?"

She wanted to say yes, but couldn't speak before a sob shattered from her throat. She doubled over, struggling to catch her breath. Her mind filled with nothing but desperation.

Hold on. Be strong. Can't let go.

"We're on our way, sweetheart." The line went dead.

CHAPTER SEVEN

Thursday Night, Nine Hours Underground

LINC CLOSED HIS EYES. He was exhausted. Beyond exhausted. He'd been awake far too long. Since Julia had moved out, he'd done little more than doze. And then today.

Even breathing taxed his strength. The air was stifling and hard to pull into his lungs. And cold. He shivered in response to his own thoughts as well as the temperature.

Gabe snored loudly a few feet away. The kid kept mumbling in his sleep. Robert was silent, which told Linc that the man was as awake as he was. Zach and Mike sat near Casey, talking softly, though Linc couldn't tell if it was to each other or to the injured man.

Sleep was tempting, but fear had so far made it impossible.

"You want to sleep?" Mike's voice cut across the dark shadows. "I'll keep an eye on the meter."

"Probably should get some rest," Linc admitted despite the fact that every atom of his body was fighting to stay awake. "You okay?" Linc recalled Mike's emotions from earlier.

"I'm fine," Mike assured him.

"Give me a couple hours then I'll spell you."

Mike stood and came over to get the meter from Linc's pack. "I'll wake you."

Since they'd settled here, Linc had spent little time doing anything but thinking, worrying and praying. Now he lay down, closed his eyes and willed sleep to come. But although he was exhausted, his brain wouldn't shut off.

"I can handle it, you know." Mike seemed to notice he wasn't sleeping. "You can relax."

"It's not that I don't trust you." Linc sat up and leaned back on the cold, hard wall. "My mind's too busy."

"I know. I can't stop thinking about Rachel. This pregnancy's been hard on her. She's been sick a lot."

"Been there, done that." Linc fought the smile. Julia hadn't been sick often with their baby but when she was...

"Yeah, there isn't much I can do. I feel so helpless. Nearly makes me lose *my* lunch."

"Sucks, doesn't it?" Linc felt memories tug at him. He couldn't let the hurt of remembering Julia's brief pregnancy come back to him. Not now. Lord, not now.

Why did the past keep reaching out from the depths of the dark to ensnare him? Was this what they meant by your life flashing in front of your eyes before you died?

Mike's memories of Rachel were here and now, but the memories that grabbed Linc were from a long way back. From a time before the world fell apart.

The first time he'd taken care of Julia when she was sick had been back in college. She'd been drunk. They'd had a fight, about what he had no clue now, but her roommate had gotten the bright idea to help her drink her troubles away. Linc had been left to clean up the mess—literally.

Julia had called him, making no sense as she'd had a few drinks. Worried, he'd gone over to her dorm room, and even totally wasted, she'd turned him on. She'd tasted like sweet lemonade, denied passion and just plain hot woman. He'd liked it.

Just as he'd been about to kiss her again, she'd pulled away and her face had paled as her eyes grew wide.

He remembered picking her up, throwing her over his shoulder and praying she wouldn't puke on him before he got her to the restroom down the hall.

He'd broken into a run and slammed through the ladies' room door—no one had been inside, thank goodness. He hadn't cared about what anyone else might have thought.

What had worried him was someone seeing Julia like this and having her be humiliated.

He'd lowered Julia to her feet in the nearest stall… just in time for the hard lemonades she'd drunk to return to this world.

Holding her hair back, he'd waited and soothed her. She'd finally sunk to the floor and tried to curl up on the cool tile. He'd joined her and held her, gently rocking the misery away. He remembered pulling off a length of toilet paper and wiping her mouth as she stared back at him through tear-filled eyes. She'd looked like hell, not the pretty, confident woman he knew.

He couldn't help but smile thinking about her reaction

when she'd realized where they were. He'd dried her tears before lifting her into his arms and heading back to her room. She'd snuggled close, and he'd tried to ignore his body's reaction to the soft woman plastered across his body.

He'd failed miserably.

Thursday Night, 11:30 p.m.

THE NOISE OF THE FAMILY members in the tent faded away. "You go ahead and cry it out." Mamie's aged, gnarled hand curled gently around Julia's tightly clasped fingers. She didn't remember the old woman sitting down. "It won't fix anything, but it might soften some of those sharp edges cutting into your heart."

She might have laughed if the sentiment hadn't fit so well.

"Why, when my Reggie was trapped back in…"

Julia tried to focus on the old woman's words, suddenly aware of how many people had been through times like this. Maybe she should listen to someone else's memories for a while instead of letting her own torment her. A nice idea not easily done.

Even as she listened, she realized how difficult life had been for Mamie, for so many coal-mining families. A small window opened into Linc's past, a past he'd hidden from her.

She couldn't help wondering why everything had to be so hard. She knew people had always thought life was too easy for her. Born into a rich family, she hadn't had to worry about her father going to a dangerous job like

Linc's father had at the mines. No, her father hadn't had that excuse.

But he'd left her just the same. A day full of business meetings and evenings of cocktail parties and charity events hadn't allowed much time for a child. She'd had to fight for every bit of attention she'd gotten from her parents.

Many of her friends had turned to outrageous and even dangerous behaviors to get their parents to notice them. She'd known that wouldn't work with her father. So she'd gone the other way. Doing everything perfectly. She'd been so good in school her classmates were often jealous. Boys, like Linc, took a perverse pleasure in trying to shake her out of that perfection. Eventually they'd all moved on. All except Linc.

"You got a good man down there?" Mamie's voice broke into her thoughts.

Nodding, Julia wiped her eyes with her fingers. Linc was a good man. It wasn't all his fault that their marriage was a mess. Her eyes blurred again. Mamie handed her an old-fashioned, embroidered handkerchief that was almost too pretty to use.

"It's washable." Mamie seemed to read her mind. Julia laughed and dried her eyes.

"Any little ones?"

How many times had that question been asked of her or Linc? Every time, rather than the pain easing, it only grew worse.

She could only shake her head in response. She used the handkerchief anew. "We've tried."

Mamie didn't push but didn't turn away, either. Julia

looked up and met the woman's time-worn gaze. There was no pity, just sympathy and perhaps an understanding she might never know the details of.

"I...I had a miscarriage."

"I'm sorry, dear."

"Me, too. The doctors never really knew why, and I haven't been able to get pregnant since." She didn't add that the chances were slim since she hardly saw Linc. Their troubled marriage had cost them so much. She blinked away the tears that blurred the sight of Mamie's hand folded over hers.

Julia couldn't remember the last time she'd talked about the baby, but something about Mamie inspired trust.

Linc certainly wouldn't discuss it. Past arguments came back to cut her heart again. Her requests that they see a fertility specialist. His adamant refusals even to discuss it. "What's meant to be will be," he'd said over and over. She'd finally stopped bringing it up and the baby that had never really been now ceased to be.

Suddenly, voices sounded outside the tent, startling them both. Julia stood and Mamie followed, holding tightly to Julia's supporting arm.

Patrick Kelly strode into the tent, two other men right behind him. While Patrick wore a hard hat and his shirt was smudged with dirt, the other two men were covered in grime. Their teeth looked inordinately white against their coal-blackened skin. She couldn't tell if they were smiling or not.

Patrick climbed up onto a folding chair in order to

be seen by everyone and to get their attention. Silence immediately descended.

Julia stood tall. She might cry and she might hurt, but she was determined to face this with as much strength as she could muster.

She didn't let go of Mamie's hand, though.

"Everyone." Patrick lifted his hands as if in supplication. "We have some good news. First, the ventilation system is working. We aren't getting any readings of high gas."

A round of applause met that bit of information. Julia stood, waiting for the rest. Dreading anything but news that they'd found them.

"I'm not going to lie to you. I already promised that," he began. Julia groaned. Just say it, she wanted to scream.

The news wasn't as bad as she'd anticipated. One of the pumps had given out, but they were shipping another one in from just across the county line.

"We've located the cavern where the men are most likely trapped." Patrick paused, waiting for the crowd to stop murmuring.

One of the men with Patrick moved forward and launched into an explanation of how they were going to try something different as Patrick stepped down. Julia understood about half of it, and wasn't sure she wanted to know the how of it. She just wanted them to tell her *when*. To tell her *if* there was anything to even hope for.

"I know what you're thinking, Jack." Patrick met Jack Sinclair's gaze. Jack was standing at the front of the group. "We do have a solution. Something they didn't have back in eighty-five when the Wilson Mine blew." Memories of that failed rescue still haunted so many in the mining industry.

"Thank God," Jack whispered.

"There's a type of drill they used up in Quecreek. It goes down from the surface straight into the cavern. It'll carve a hole in the earth big enough to pull them out."

Julia recalled the heroics of Quecreek. The round-the-clock digging, the drill that broke and was fixed by a team within hours. Every mining disaster since then had fallen short of Quecreek's success. She tried not to think about that.

"We don't have it here," Jack pointed out.

"It's on the way. It'll be here in three hours."

"Three hours?" Rachel Sinclair abruptly sat on a metal folding chair. She hooked an arm over her belly, hugging her unborn child. "They could be dead by then."

"No." Patrick shook his head. "We've calculated it. We think they'll be fine then...if they're fine now."

What he didn't say, every face in the room showed. But *were* they okay now? That was the million-dollar question. One none of them could—or would—answer.

"This is the only solution we can come up with right now," Patrick continued. "When the drill gets here, we're going to set it up on the other side of the north ridge. You won't be able to see it from here."

"Why there?" Rita asked.

"They're in the back half of the mine," her husband

told her, his voice thick with fear. "They ain't coming out the mouth."

"You're right, Jack," Patrick continued. "We can't get to them from the current opening to the mine. They'll be coming up through a rescue shaft we'll be drilling. We'll keep you posted."

While no one broke into cheers, there were no breakdowns either. Everyone just stood waiting, as if maybe there would be more and yet knowing there wasn't.

"I'll be back as soon as I know anything." With that, Patrick and his men were gone.

Julia sank back to her seat. Mamie sat more slowly.

"Well, that's that." The older woman looked suddenly very tired.

"Have you eaten anything?"

"No."

"We need to keep up our strength." Now who was taking care of whom?

"My thoughts exactly." A man's voice startled them both. Julia turned to find Trish and her father standing behind them. They each held steaming bowls. Walt handed one to Mamie and the other to Julia. They pulled up chairs to form a small circle. No one ate much, just stirred and sipped the warm soup.

No one spoke. There wasn't much to say, but for the first time in years, Julia didn't feel so alone.

Thursday Night, Ten Hours Underground

LINC AWOKE SUDDENLY. It took him ages to remember where he was and to fight the panic that held a hard grip on his chest. He stood, needing to move, to get the dream out of his head. He'd been holding Julia, their bodies close.

He shook his head to banish the images, then looked around at the other men. "Where's Mike?" he asked them all, knowing Robert was the most likely to respond.

Robert was his predictable self. "He went out to stretch his legs a while ago. He's determined to find a ventilation pipe or something."

"How long ago?"

Gabe checked his watch. "Ten minutes."

They hadn't talked much about trying to find something to tap on. Just like building the walls, it was an old mining standby. They wouldn't know if anyone heard them, or even if the pipe was still connected to anything, but miners were trained to do it anyway.

If the rescue crews had the seismic equipment out they'd hear it. Seven raps for a live crew of seven. It was universal and anyone in the industry—or who knew anything about mining—knew what it meant.

Mike was the most desperate to get out. Linc grabbed his lamp. The battery was low but he had to risk it. Mike had been gone too long.

He looked around for the meter but didn't see it. Mike must have taken it with him. *Damn.* He picked up his breathing apparatus, hoping he wouldn't find any bad gas, but prepared in case he did.

Linc trekked down the narrow incline, moving in a hunched duck walk. The pace was slower but one they all did automatically now.

"Mike?" he called as he reached the end of the tunnel

where the vent system came down. In the faint glow of the lamp, he saw a form huddled beside what looked like a mangled pipe.

As he drew closer, he saw the ball-peen hammer Ryan had found earlier. It was poised in the air, ready to strike. The hammer hit once, twice, seven times. The peal echoed in the chamber, almost harsh before the walls swallowed the sound.

"Mike?" Linc called softly. Startled, the young man spun around. The tracks of dampness on his cheeks glistened in the light.

"What happened?" Linc hurried to him.

"They've got to find us. They got to." Mike's voice hitched. "My kid's coming soon. I gotta be there. I can't leave Rach to do it all by herself. I just can't."

Mike's words hit him like a punch to the gut. In that instant, he heard the voice of the man kneeling beside him—and his father's voice echoing across time.

Had his father spoken similar words into that other dark cavern? Had he done as Mike was doing, desperately raging to escape and return to his family?

The anger Linc had carried for years—since his sixteen-year-old self had blamed his father for leaving them—took a fatal blow. All at once he could focus on the man he'd loved and joked with. The man who had taken his sons fishing, thinking it was the thing to do, despite the fact he hated to fish.

Fiascos of the past suddenly became warm memories of a man trying to be a better father than his had ever been.

"Mike?" Linc squeezed the other man's shoulder.

"You need to rest. We'll all take turns doing this. My turn now." He took the hammer and rapped out the seven-beat tune just as Mike had done. "Go rest."

Linc took the gas meter from Mike's hand and put it back on his pack, where it would stay. He checked it and found the gauge indicated a slight elevation.

Time was no longer on their side.

CHAPTER EIGHT

Friday Morning, 7:00 a.m.

ONCE AGAIN, JULIA STOOD at the opening of the tent, staring out across the wide valley. She and the other family members had been stuck in this moth-eaten tent for what seemed like ages. It had been less than a full day.

They were close enough to see what was happening at the mouth of the mine, but far enough to keep them from interfering with the activities.

She paced, feeling the cool morning breeze on her face, smelling the rich odor of the newly churned earth. Earth that separated her from Linc, the man she'd been married to for seven years. Her breath caught as the day registered. If she thought about that too much she'd lose control. She had to do something. She turned toward the entrance, propelled by frustration. She intended to run down into the valley and help with the rescue efforts.

Shirley Wise's low voice broke into Julia's thoughts. "Getting in the way won't help." Julia looked over to see the older woman blowing on a steaming cup of coffee.

"I wasn't going to—"

"Yes, you were." The woman smiled, not warmly,

and tentatively sipped the brew. "You were about to head down into that valley where all those men will focus more on protecting you than on saving our men." The accusation was sharp and direct.

Julia wanted to deny it, then decided not to bother. She didn't have the energy to argue right now. Why didn't Shirley like her? Maybe she'd learned of Julia's background as a mine-owner's daughter. That animosity was generations in the making and she'd faced it many times in her life. The only other thing Julia could think of was the incident with Ryan. She and Shirley had only crossed paths a half-dozen times since she and Linc had moved here, but nothing else came to mind.

"Shirley, what did I ever do to make you dislike me?" Julia spoke her thoughts before thinking.

"Why…I…I don't dislike you." Shirley didn't look Julia in the eye, which was the first clue that she was lying.

"Maybe *dislike* is the wrong word. But you definitely don't trust me."

Shirley took a deep swallow of her coffee and Julia was surprised she didn't wince. It had to be hot. Finally, she met Julia's gaze. "You shake things up. You're the kind of person who comes in and makes changes."

"What's wrong with that?" Julia couldn't think of what she'd done that might have had any direct impact on Shirley or Gabe Wise.

"There's plenty wrong with that." Shirley's voice rose, then, looking over her shoulder at the crowd behind them, she took a deep, calming breath. "Boys in this town have been going to the mines to help their families for decades."

Ah, so this *was* about Ryan. "Just because it's always been done, doesn't make it right."

"Humph." Shirley drank again, her eyes narrowed toward the horizon. "It's not up to you to decide that. You've done enough damage. Don't you do anything that puts my husband in more danger." Without waiting for Julia to respond, Shirley sank back into the confines of the tent, leaving Julia alone to stare after her in shock.

In one aspect, Shirley was right. Julia had never been the type to sit back and accept the status quo. She'd always questioned and wanted to make things better for people. She didn't think she'd ever been militant or pushy, but she did prod and work at something until she got what she wanted. Obviously, that had upset people.

She couldn't regret it, though. When it came to Ryan, or any of the other boys she taught, she'd do the same thing all over again. Maybe if they'd listened to her, Ryan wouldn't be trapped right now, possibly dead.

Shirley's warning not to interfere warred with Julia's panic and the need she felt to do something to help. She turned away from the view of the valley, away from the temptation of the rescue effort, and went back inside. Shirley was right. Those workers would try to take care of her, and they couldn't afford that distraction.

But she had to do *something*. The soft patter of raindrops hit the canvas and she watched tiny rivers fall down the plastic windows in the sides of the tent.

Struggling against despair, she pulled her gaze from

the quickly dampening world to look around the make-shift room.

There were six other women here whose men were trapped below. Friends and relatives grouped together around the others, whispering and trying to keep their words unheard.

Julia was the only one here alone. Her parents were on their way from Philadelphia, or at least that's what they'd said. She glanced at her watch. They should arrive in about an hour. But they weren't here yet.

She'd always thought she wanted to be on her own. To be independent. Since meeting Linc, she'd forgotten how lonely alone could be. In the past few days, in that empty apartment, her anger had kept the loneliness at bay. Now she felt it circling her.

"Be careful what you wish for." She heard a voice that sounded too much like Linc's, as if his ghost were whispering on the wind.

"No." She almost screamed, afraid that thinking such a thing would somehow make it true.

Whether it was the cold of the rain, or the chill of her own thoughts, she shivered and wished for warmth, for someone's arms to hold her.

Could she and Linc fix what was wrong between them? Would he ever hold her again? The thought hurt and she choked back a gasp. She realized that, over time, she'd taken his presence, his touch, *him* for granted. Once, when their relationship was young, she'd desperately wanted him and his touch. She'd have done just about anything to get it.

Now, she'd walked away from everything.

Friday Morning, Seventeen Hours Underground

LINC SAT AT THE EDGE of the shelter. The others were nearby, but he felt alone.

He pulled the heavy helmet off his head. He wore it often, but not all day like the other guys. It strained his neck and shoulders. His hair was damp from sweat and he raked his fingers through it, trying to ease the grimy feeling. What he wouldn't give for a shower right now.

He must look like hell, but what did it matter? He shifted, trying to get more comfortable. Once again his thoughts turned to Julia.

Closing his eyes, he leaned his head back. He rubbed his hands over his face, hoping to wipe off some of the grit, as well as to wipe the hurt from his features.

Now, when he was staring his mortality in the eyes, he kept forgetting that he was angry with her.

That she'd lied to him.

That she'd left him.

He needed to hang on to that anger because what if she wasn't up there waiting when he got out of here? What was he supposed to do then?

How was he supposed to rebuild his life without her in it? He couldn't return to the emptiness he'd faced after she'd left. But would he even have a choice?

After she'd lost the baby he'd tried to help her. Like taking her away to that cabin for a long weekend. Time had passed. He'd thought she was better. Obviously she wasn't, if she'd switched jobs. What had she said? Something about not being around the little kids.

She hadn't even told him at the time. Maybe she'd

been like him. Unsure what to say, knowing that anything said at that moment would have far-reaching consequences.

What had happened to them? She'd completely changed her life without even bothering to ask his opinion or discuss it with him. When had she grown so distant?

He'd always thought she leaned on him, counted on him. He'd always wanted to be there for her.

But apparently she didn't need him anymore.

"Help me out here!" Gabe's voice brought Linc abruptly back to the present. Casey was thrashing in his sleep. Robert grabbed his arms, and Linc helped the older man stabilize his injured leg again. They were all panting from the exertion when they were finished. Casey settled back to sleep and Linc slumped against the wall.

The arguments and rift between him and Julia returned to where it should be…a lifetime ago, maybe even someone else's lifetime. If—no, when—they got out of here, he had a hell of a lot of work ahead.

Friday Morning—9:00 a.m.

"WHERE'S MY LITTLE GIRL?"

Julia cringed at her father's bellow. At twenty-nine, she wasn't anyone's little girl, but subtlety had never been Raymond Alton's strong suit, and now was no exception. She sagged a little with relief that her parents were finally here and she didn't have to be alone—then she tensed up again in anticipation of the baggage they brought with them.

Her parents had seldom hugged her. They'd been too busy, too distant, too uncomfortable. So she was shocked when her father swept her into a strong embrace. She heard her mother's anxious voice and felt her feather-light touch caressing her hair.

Julia closed her eyes and let herself sink into their ministrations. She let herself believe, for just a while, as she had when she was a child, that Mom and Dad could fix everything.

Her eyes burned and the ache in her throat intensified. She knew that if she started crying now, she might never stop. She fought the temptation and pulled back to look at her parents. It had been months since she'd seen them. They looked older, worried. Was this too much for them? They were both in their sixties.

"What's happening? Fill us in." Her father guided her to a chair and sat down beside her. Her mother, Eleanor, absently rubbed her shoulders. She'd forgotten that her mother used to do that when she was a child. It felt good. What else had she forgotten?

Instead of letting her thoughts go down that path, she focused on her father's question. "We don't know much. There was a cave-in and Linc was down with a crew on the second shift. They hadn't been down long."

"Gas?" he asked softly. They all knew he meant the deadly methane that plagued all coal-mining operations.

"They don't know."

His curse was soft, not meant for her to hear, but

spoken aloud, nonetheless. "Let me see if I can get some answers." He started to stand.

"Dad. Please." She recalled Shirley's animosity and grabbed his arm to stop him. She wasn't sure it was a good idea for him to be throwing his weight around. Not yet anyway.

"What?" Raymond looked at her hand, a strange, surprised look in his eyes.

"This isn't your mine, nor your operation. We're one of the families this time," she whispered and regretted each word when his shoulders slumped as if in defeat— or as if some weight had been settled there. "Just be here with me for now, okay?"

"We're here for you, sweetheart." Her mother slipped an arm around her shoulders. "Whatever you need from us, we're here."

The catch in her mother's voice and the sheen in her father's eyes combined was nearly too much. Julia and her parents had had their troubles, but all that seemed forgotten now. "I don't know if I can do this," she said.

"You can and you will." Raymond sat up straighter. "The Altons have weathered plenty of storms. We'll get through this one." His bravado and certainty—a certainty she'd always found arrogant before—gave her the extra nudge she needed. She leaned into her mother's shoulder and said something she doubted she'd ever said to them before. "Thank you." She was surprised at how easily she could turn to them.

Just then, Patrick Kelly and the two other men

came back in. Their eyes were bloodshot in their coal-blackened faces.

Her heart sank and she appreciated her parents' timing. Here it was. The news they'd all been expecting. Thank God her parents were here. They'd pick up the pieces.

She knew she couldn't.

CHAPTER NINE

Friday Afternoon, Twenty-Four Hours Underground

THEY LEFT THE LAMP from Casey's hard hat turned on. Linc had extinguished his own, just as the others had, to save the batteries. Casey was finally quiet, the pain of his injuries rendering him oblivious to his surroundings. A good thing for him right now.

They took turns sitting with him. Linc kept his thoughts to himself, but as he approached the injured man, he found himself holding his breath. *Please God, don't let me find him dead.*

"Is he any better?" He expected Gabe to look up when he approached. Instead, the older man simply shook his head and stood. The darkness swallowed Gabe as he slowly walked away. Linc settled down at Casey's side.

"He's taking the responsibility for all of this on his shoulders." Robert's disembodied voice echoed Linc's thoughts.

"None of this is Gabe's fault." Linc struggled to keep the suspicion out of his voice. "Unless he did something he wasn't supposed to." Someone must have done something—mines didn't just collapse for no reason. What, he didn't know. He wasn't sure if he'd ever know.

"You don't get how it works down here, do you?" Robert stepped forward and into the dim circle of light. Anger and shadows contorted his face. His hands were fisted at his sides.

Linc had run up against miners hostile to inspectors before. Nothing new there, but it frustrated him that Robert couldn't set it aside now. He held on to his desire to vent his frustration. Did the others feel the same way?

"Oh, I get it." Linc stood, not willing to give the other man the advantage of looming over him. "I get that the mine owners send good men like all of you down here to bust your butts. And for what?" He stepped toward Robert. "Nothing but obscenely low amounts of money."

"It's more than that." Robert took a step forward, too. "It's a way of life. It's the backbone of the energy industry that keeps this whole damn country running."

"You actually buy the crap they shovel at company meetings?"

"I buy. I believe. It's who I am. It's who we all are. You aren't one of us and you'll never understand."

"I understand plenty." Linc's voice lowered as his throat tightened. "I grew up with the mines. My father was just like you. Just like Gabe. He believed it all, too."

Robert didn't speak but continued to glare.

"Until two tons of rock fell on him and his whole crew."

Still, Robert remained silent. Linc wanted him to

understand his position, probably as much as Robert believed in his own convictions.

"Then you dishonor him and his death working as an inspector," Robert said.

Linc clenched his jaw and forced himself not to shout. "You're treading on dangerous ground."

"And? You can speak your mind, but I can't? You're a stranger here. This is my world."

"Hey." Gabe appeared in the small circle of light. "You two cut it out. You got problems with each other, deal with them later."

What if they didn't have later? Linc wondered, but held his tongue. He respected Gabe too much.

Taking a deep breath and letting it out, Linc tried to purge his system of the anger. He'd always been quick to react—or overreact, as Julia often reminded him.

Robert disappeared into the darkness, and Linc heard the rustle as he settled on the other side of the chamber. Gabe looked at Linc, but didn't say a word. His expression was unreadable. Censure or sympathy? "It's my turn to send the signal." Gabe turned with a shrug and headed toward the pipe.

Seconds later, seven peals of metal on metal broke the ungodly quiet.

Linc sat back down. *Was* he an outsider? While he fought the idea, it took hold and refused to let go. What bothered him most was the realization that his father probably would have agreed with Robert. He'd been a company man through and through.

Closing his eyes, Linc shoved aside Robert's accusations, his father's memory and this whole damned situation. Lord, he was tired, but just as on every night since Julia had left him, he couldn't sleep. Why couldn't he just let go? She was the one who'd lied. The one who had walked out.

He pressed the heels of his hands to his eyes, letting the pressure drain out the ache.

Why did he still want her? Was he such a fool that he let her take advantage of him?

What else had she lied about? He ignored that can of worms. Was she right now sitting at the house, waiting for him to die so she could avoid the hassle of a divorce?

He groaned, letting his anger replace the fear of dying.

But even his anger at the situation, at Robert, or with Julia couldn't keep her image from forming in his mind. An image that all too easily morphed into something different.

Instead of yelling at him, she was smiling. Instead of seething at her, he was reaching out, touching the soft copper waves of her hair.

He wanted to hate her, wanted to forget what it felt like to love her, but he couldn't.

His life was entwined with hers. He'd been the first to make love to her. She'd given him her virginity on a hot summer night in the dew-cooled grasses of Hamilton Park.

She'd looked so incredibly beautiful as she lost herself in passion. If he was going to die, he wanted that to be his last image.

They'd made love hundreds of times in the years since then. It had never lost its magic.

Never.

Friday Afternoon, 3:00 p.m.

JULIA WATCHED AS Patrick Kelly came into the tent with two men that she hadn't seen before.

Patrick was a big man, with a receding hairline and wide green eyes. The other men easily rivaled him in height.

So far, he'd stuck to his word and hadn't "blown smoke up their asses." He'd admitted that he might not always have the answers they wanted, but he *would* have answers.

Julia stayed where she was, though several of the other family members moved closer. The tent wasn't so vast that she couldn't hear him. She felt her mother's hand tighten on her shoulder and saw her father sit up a little straighter.

"The ventilation drill is about a third of the way down to where we think they are." A third of the way in what—Julia glanced down at her watch—twenty-four hours? At this rate, how could they possibly break through in time?

Patrick paused as if not wanting to share the rest. Everyone held their breath. "I told you I'd be honest with you and I'm keeping that promise." He paused. "We've got water rising on the east side. Jim here is in charge of the pumps, and we've started all of them. We've got more pumps coming in from the Griffin Mine

and the White Water operations. They'll be here sometime before midnight." Jim nodded as if to confirm what
Patrick was telling them.

Julia felt for them. Patrick's heart was clearly in his
eyes. He'd been in the mines for years himself. Of everyone, he knew what they were really up against. The
fact that his voice held an edge of panic didn't do much
to reassure the rest of them.

Voices erupted around her, but Julia could only stare
blankly ahead. Could it get any worse? The small group
of men left as quickly as they'd arrived, letting them all
absorb the news. Julia pulled the numbness back over
herself as she felt her mother move to stand close beside
her.

"You need to eat something, dear."

Eleanor Alton was definitely out of her element here.
There were no committees or activities to organize. Just
sitting and waiting. Julia was having a tough time with
it and her mother was surely nearing her limit. She
couldn't recall her mother ever being still this long.

Julia stood and went to get more coffee. She'd had
enough caffeine to last her the rest of her life, but she
didn't want anything to eat.

At the back corner of the tent, she found a quiet place
to sit, momentarily. It was less crowded as three families
had returned home—at least for a little while. Those
who'd stayed were silently waiting for the next report.

The very thought of going home to the dark and
empty house alone sent shivers up Julia's spine. But
what if she eventually had to? What if after all this

effort by all these volunteers and rescue workers, they weren't able to save them?

Her stomach was in knots, but rather than give in to her fears, she stood and paced some more. It helped ease the tight muscles but even so, the emotions hovered nearby, waiting to pounce.

Rita Sinclair sat on a folding chair near the makeshift podium. Her crochet hook moved quickly and several hanks of yarn were nestled in a basket at her feet. The light flashed on the metal hook as she added to her swatch.

"What are you making?" Julia asked.

Rita smiled weakly and shrugged. "I don't really know, but I can't just sit. I'll go crazy."

"That helps?"

"Yeah. When Jack was hurt six years ago, he was in the hospital for weeks. My crocheting was nearly thirty feet long when I finished."

They both laughed and Julia wished she had something like that to distract herself.

"Would you like to do some?"

"Oh, I don't know how."

Rita patted the seat next to her. "I always come prepared." She reached into her bag and pulled out another hook, a little bigger than the one she used, and a bright blue skein of yarn.

"Make a loop like this." Rita took the yarn and gently guided Julia's hands through the first few stitches. "Now just keep going."

And so they sat, Rita making smooth rows of multicolored crochet and Julia building an uneven pile of blue loops.

It did help. The concentration required distracted her and the movement of her hands eased the need to get up and walk.

"I taught my eldest girl to do this when she was pregnant and on bed rest."

"Did it help her?"

"I guess. That grandbaby has enough blankets to last her till she's eight."

Julia laughed…then all the joy faded as the image of baby blankets soaked in. She knew she wasn't pregnant now. If Linc wasn't rescued…if he never came home… All the fears and regrets seemed to leap out of the shadows. What was she thinking? He might never speak to her again, much less make love to her, not just because he couldn't. More than the cave-in kept them apart. She'd never—

"Keep crocheting, child," the older woman whispered, her own needle picking up speed. "Don't give yourself time to think."

Suddenly, Julia looked up and met her mother's gaze across the tent. The past came back with a rush.

Julia had come home with a beautiful diamond on her hand and her heart plastered all over her face. She'd wakened her parents to share her news only to find them less than thrilled.

Her father's question still cut painfully across time. Did she *have* to get married?

All the sparkle had gone out of her night but the most damaging comment had come from her mother.

It hadn't been a question, but a refusal to accept a "had to get married" child.

"Don't expect me to knit any baby booties," Eleanor had snarled.

It had taken Linc weeks to get the details out of her. And several more weeks to convince her to talk to them again. They didn't have to like him, he'd said. But they were her parents and part of her. He wasn't letting her make any rash decisions.

And so while the wall wasn't as high as it could have been, it was still there, standing solidly between them, even in this cramped tent.

Eleanor walked toward her. Julia looked down, concentrating on her uneven string of looped blue yarn.

"May I?" The chair beside Julia shifted, scraping in the dirt. "Rita, isn't it? How do I do this?"

Julia looked up then, seeing her mother awkwardly grasping a crochet hook and the purple yarn Rita handed her. Both older women laughed as she struggled to get the fingering right.

But her mother was trying, Julia realized. Really, honestly trying.

Friday Afternoon, Twenty-Six Hours Underground

"SIT YOUR ASS DOWN, OLD MAN," Zach said as he half carried Gabe over to where Linc sat next to Casey. Linc scooted out of the way, then knelt beside Gabe after Zach stepped back.

Both of them switched on their helmet lights. Gabe

squinted in the sudden brightness and Linc turned his off. "What happened?" Linc looked at Zach.

"He hunched over back there. Nearly fell on his face."

"Chest hurts," Gabe whispered.

Ah, shit. Linc closed his eyes, then opened them again to look at the older miner more closely. It was hard to tell what his coloring was like in the poor light. His eyes were closed and the lines around his eyes and mouth had deepened. Linc grabbed his wrist and found his pulse strong, but quick.

"Any gas?" Zach looked pointedly at the meter on Linc's pack.

They both looked down at the dials. "Nope. No changes," Linc said. He thought he heard everyone sigh in relief. "Put your air on anyway, Gabe." He helped the older man with his equipment. "Put Casey's on, too. We probably should have done that before. He could use the help."

"Good idea." Zach helped the semiconscious man put on the breathing apparatus. He did seem to relax a little. Maybe he'd rest more now. He needed to if he was going to survive that wound to his leg.

"What's the matter with Gabe?" Ryan's panic filled the small chamber, making everyone shift uncomfortably.

Footsteps told Linc everyone was there. Robert and Mike walked up to stand beside Ryan.

"He just needs to rest." Linc had basic first-aid training, but that was all he could offer them. He turned to the others. Each of them looked as afraid as he felt. "We could all probably use some rest." He didn't think about the nap he'd just tried to take, the one that had led to thoughts of Julia.

He scooted over next to Gabe. Ryan followed suit and settled in beside him. Robert headed over to the opposite end.

Lined up there against the wall, they all stared straight ahead. Zach left his light on and its beam bounced back off the wall, painting them in a distorted glow.

The silence was heavy. Thick with threat.

And then they heard it. A sound that hadn't been there before. A whining, grinding, brutal sound.

Something, someone, was finally coming for them. Hope flickered for an instant. Then Gabe lapsed into a coughing jag.

Would they get here soon enough?

CHAPTER TEN

Friday Afternoon, 5:00 p.m.

JULIA HAD REACHED A POINT with the crochet where she could keep going without constantly watching her hands. Granted, it was just a single row that seemed to stretch out for miles, but she felt better, calmer, as if she were *doing* something.

She glanced around the room, seeing that one of the families who had left earlier had returned, looking freshly showered but no less haggard. Beyond them, her father sat on a folding chair, his elbows resting on his knees. Jack Sinclair faced him and they were deep in discussion.

She panicked for a moment, not trusting her father's responses. She couldn't recall when she'd ever seen her father sit and talk with one of the workers without an argument erupting. But while Jack was talking with great animation, her father seemed to be listening. Still concerned, she stood. "Excuse me." She set her crochet down and headed toward the men, just in case.

"Raising kids sure is tough," Jack was saying.

Her father nodded and Julia held back, about to turn away. She was relieved that they weren't arguing about the cave-in or the industry or such.

"Don't I know it. I wonder what's easier, girls or boys? I only had the one daughter," her father admitted.

"Probably neither," Jack said. Both men laughed. "I never wanted my boys underground."

Julia was shocked. Jack had been so adamant when she was trying to keep Ryan in school. His comment surprised her. Then he clarified. "Both boys came to me and wanted to do it. I might not like it, but I'll support anything they want to do."

"Even after this?"

There was a long pause. "Yeah," Jack admitted softly. "If they really want to, I'll support them. I'll just drink a little more Maalox." Both men laughed again, but with much less humor.

Julia backed up, hurrying away from the touching realization of how much Jack loved his sons. Enough to let them do something he didn't want for them.

She didn't stick around to hear her father's response. She didn't want to know what dreams he'd had for her and how much she'd disappointed him.

Friday Afternoon, Twenty-Seven Hours Underground

THE DISTANT GRINDING SOUND was so faint that, if Linc had been talking or sleeping, it would have been lost. But it was constant.

"What's that?" Ryan whispered.

Gabe was stronger now and shifted around as if trying to get closer to the stone wall. "It ain't coming from the tunnel. It's overhead."

Linc tried to read Gabe's expression but the man's eyes were shadowed. He wasn't smiling.

"What does it mean?" Ryan really was at a disadvantage. He was way too young and inexperienced to be trapped like this.

"It means the next chamber is full of either water or shale. They can't get to us that way," Gabe said.

"We're going to die here?" Ryan's voice cracked.

"No." Gabe put all of his determination into that one word. "It means they're coming for us from the top."

Two hundred feet straight down through solid rock. Linc shook his head. It wouldn't work. If it did, would they beat the elements, rising water or gases, which everyone knew were risk factors in a mine?

The battices the crew had put up helped hold in some of their body heat but the mine was only fifty-eight degrees. Even the smallest and worst-equipped mines had canvas battices stored throughout the tunnels. If the gases rose, the canvas would block it somewhat. The cool rock against his back, and the lack of activity, made Linc shiver. The men sat together, subconsciously seeking each other's warmth.

"It's cold." Ryan's teeth chattered. Even in the faint light, Linc saw Mike scoot closer to his brother. He did the same. Of them all, Ryan was the smallest and probably had a greater challenge staying warm.

"Get up and move around to get the blood flowing," Robert suggested. "Just don't overdo it."

Linc had to admit that was a good idea. Ryan must have thought so, too, as he struggled to stand. "I'll go beat the pipe again. Maybe this time they'll hear us."

"Maybe they will." Mike's voice held an edge Linc couldn't quite identify. Hope strangled by fear? He shook his head. He needed to get some sleep. His mind was fading.

"Go to the pipe." Gabe's voice was soft but as authoritative as ever. "But don't go messing with shit along the way."

"Yeah, I know." Ryan's smile was almost audible as he swept the canvas aside and slipped through the opening. Linc sensed Mike tensing as they watched the boy leave.

"He'll be okay," Linc reassured Mike.

"You don't know my little brother very well, do you?" Mike said with a smile of his own.

"I have some idea. My wife mentioned him and I've heard your dad talk."

"Yeah, I know about that. If it means anything, she gave it a good shot."

"What do you mean?"

"None of us wanted him down here. Dad always gets bent out of shape when someone tries to tell him what to do, so he overreacted when she talked to Ryan. I wish he'd listened to her."

"She'll be glad to hear that. I'll be sure and tell her."

"Yeah. That'd be nice."

The silence settled back in place. Linc hoped he'd get the chance to tell Julia just that. Then they'd all be out of here.

Linc shifted and something hard dug into his hip. He reached into his pocket and couldn't help but laugh. Fat lot of good his truck keys would do him down here. All he could use them for now was jingling in his pocket to keep him awake.

"Why didn't you leave those up top?" Mike asked.

"Habit," he admitted. He didn't want to think about what they opened. Things, places, "stuff" he might never see again. When archaeologists dug up his body in a few million years, would they even know what keys were?

He thought about tossing them into the darkness. Instead, he shoved them back into his pocket, hoping he'd need them soon. Real soon.

"Hey." Ryan's alarmed voice came from the other side of the battice. His hat lamp cast a bouncing shadow on the canvas just before he pulled it aside.

"What's up?" Robert stood and walked over to the opening. "What did you find?"

"Nothing good." The kid turned around and pointed in the direction of his light beam. "There's water rising up near the first break."

"Damn it," Gabe swore. "Fast or slow?"

"Slow—maybe a couple of inches so far."

Cautious relief whispered through them all. What damage a cave-in didn't accomplish, water would.

"They'd better be digging for us fast." Ryan's voice broke as he settled back down. The boy had been strong up until now, something Linc wasn't so sure he'd have been able to do at that age.

"We've got plenty of time," Linc reassured him, knowing he was just as much reassuring himself. And maybe a few of the others.

"Keep an eye on it," Gabe said weakly.

"Let's set a mark." Robert disappeared into the darkness. Linc knew he'd find a stick or pole and put it in the water. They'd mark the level. Now every time someone went to bang on the pipe, they'd check the water level, as well.

Robert returned and settled back down. "It's not much, yet."

Casey moaned in his sleep.

"We need to get him out of here." Robert's frustration was clear.

"We *all* need to get out of here," Mike stated. No one spoke again for a long time. The silence itself was heavy and thick, just like the walls that trapped them.

Linc shifted position and the keys jangled in his pockets. Yep. He was still alive. Still awake.

But for how long?

"I'm hungry." Ryan's statement interrupted his morbid thoughts. "Can we have that lunch now?"

Linc had forgotten about the battered lunch box Ryan had found earlier.

"Might as well," Gabe said.

"Cool."

Linc heard him working to pry open the beat-up metal box. The lid groaned loudly.

"Who wants an apple?" Ryan held up the Granny Smith in the faint light. "And a…cheese sandwich?" He lifted the foil-wrapped sandwich. "Who drinks two Mountain Dews?"

"Just split it up, kid." Robert's tone was gruff. "We can do without the editorial."

Linc saw Ryan throw Robert an offended look, but wisely the kid kept his words to himself.

"Good job, kid." Gabe patted Ryan's shoulder as the boy hunkered down to give him a part of the sandwich.

"I'd even eat a school lunch right now." Ryan bit hungrily into his portion of the sandwich.

"That's sayin' a lot," Mike volunteered. "Little brother there never ate school lunches. Not unless Mom forced him."

"Shows how much you know. I'd go hungry those days." It actually sounded as if he was proud of that accomplishment.

Linc felt the mood of the dark chamber lift with the brotherly banter. He thought about Jace. A pang of loss shot through him. Nothing had been the same since Jim Holmes's death.

Linc couldn't remember the last time he'd thought about the family he'd grown up with, the one that had vanished all too early. He didn't let himself dwell on it often, but holidays and special events made it inevitable.

Linc had worked his butt off in high school to get the scholarship he'd needed to get the hell out of the small coal-mining town. He'd left, shaking the black dust off his shoes as soon as he hit the city limits.

He hadn't given a thought to his younger brother. To this day, he hadn't escaped the sense that he'd failed Jace.

Two weeks into Linc's senior year of college, Jace

had run away from home. Mom hadn't even told Linc until another two weeks had passed.

No one had seen Jace since. Linc didn't even know if his brother was alive or not. The guilt that came from not knowing settled like a stone in his gut.

Would he ever find out what had happened to Jace? Or was his brother waiting on the other side with his parents? Would Linc be seeing them all too soon?

Friday Evening, 6:30 p.m.

WAITING...WAITING...WAITING. Julia had never been patient. This interminable waiting was going to drive her insane.

Someone had brought in a stack of worn paperbacks that sat neglected on one of the tables. Julia couldn't even think straight, much less concentrate on a story.

The rain had finally stopped and faint rays of evening sunshine filtered through the trees. She couldn't resist the call of the light. The darkness of the waiting was becoming too heavy. She needed to escape.

Outside, the fading sunshine felt good. Julia turned her face toward it as she stepped outside. The sweet scent of the damp woods filled her with a hope she hadn't let herself feel in an eternity.

Julia had had enough of the crowds and the worry and the not knowing. Being outside made her feel closer to the rescue efforts, closer to something happening. Closer to Linc. She didn't dwell on that last thought long.

She'd taken only a few steps when her mother's voice stopped her. "Where are you going?"

"I...I need some air." She needed more than that but couldn't begin to explain the ache of emptiness she felt even with all these people around.

"I'll go with you."

"No."

"I'm going with you," Eleanor said more forcefully.

"Not now, Mom."

"Yes, now, Julia." The mother tone came again, the one Julia hadn't heard in years. The one Julia had dreaded as a child, the one that said she'd done something unacceptable. Julia turned and kept walking, hearing her mother's footsteps behind her. They were a good ten feet outside before she spun and faced her mother. "What is it?"

"I saw the look on your face earlier. You were remembering, too."

Eleanor stared at her, and for the first time in her memory, Julia saw uncertainty in her mother's eyes. "I realize there's a lot going on." Eleanor paused. "But that look isn't something I can let pass."

"There wasn't a look." She'd managed to hide her feelings for the past ten years. She wasn't dredging up that hurt all over again.

"I'm sorry I hurt you."

Julia was taken aback. Her mother *never* apologized. Never.

Julia felt something inside her tremble. "I don't understand." She didn't know what her mother expected. "You've never liked Linc." The years of anger came bubbling to the surface. "You never wanted me to marry him. I can't forget the things you've said and done over the years."

Eleanor sighed and paced away from Julia. Taking a deep breath, she turned back to face her daughter. "I know we weren't supportive in the beginning. For God's sake, Julia, you came bursting into our room in the middle of the night to tell us you were marrying a man we hardly knew. You didn't even give us a chance to get to know him."

"It was too uncomfortable."

"And not for us?"

"I...I never thought of it that way."

"I know that, dear, but we didn't do anything to stop you, did we?"

"Uh, no." The trembling increased. She stared at her mother, as if seeing her for the first time as an adult.

Julia shivered. The night closed in, cool and damp, and she let herself feel each aspect of it. That was better than facing the doubt that had suddenly taken hold of her soul.

"There's been so little time for us to get to know Linc. But you know what? He makes you happy, honey, and that's all we care about." Eleanor continued to pace. "We're no different from any other parents. We want what's best for you."

"You don't always know what I want."

"That's true, dear. But you aren't any better at telling us, now are you?" Eleanor was actually letting her feelings show and the hurt she exposed was strong and, Julia realized, long held.

"We've messed everything up, haven't we?" Julia

whispered and turned away. She stared out over the compound of the mine, seeing the groups of men who were taking part in the rescue effort. They seemed to be moving in slow motion. She closed her eyes. "Oh, Mom."

Julia let her head fall forward and her eyes close, hoping that her mother wouldn't see her misery. She should have known. There was no hiding this.

"Mom, we're separated. I moved out of the house last week."

Eleanor said nothing. Then slowly, gently, she laid a hand on Julia's shoulder. She didn't say anything. She still didn't do anything except lay that hand on her daughter's shoulder. Comforting. Offering.

"We've had so many troubles since—" Julia hiccuped and knew she was losing the battle. "Since I lost the baby."

Suddenly, out of nowhere, memories rushed at her. Of the weekend at the lake. Of the weeks and months Linc had tried to get home early so dinner wasn't cold. Then the angry words she'd thrown at him. Words she'd known at the time were wrong, but that she'd said nonetheless. She could see his face even now and she admitted to herself that she'd hurt him.

"I lied to him, Mom," she began. "I quit my job and didn't tell him. I couldn't work with the little kids anymore. I wanted to tell him, but I—I just didn't know how."

Eleanor remained quiet, listening, her hand slowly, gently rubbing. Soothing. She waited for Julia to continue, as though knowing she needed to purge herself of the pain.

"He was trying so hard and I just shut him out."

"You always were good at that." Eleanor's tone was oddly warm and easy. "Poor baby."

Julia lifted her head and chuckled. "Yeah." The light moment faded all too quickly. "Why didn't I pay attention? Why didn't I see what he was doing?" She turned and glanced back at the mine opening. "What if I never get to tell him I'm sorry?"

Regret and fear so strong it hurt swept over her. She looked longingly at the mine, willing the rescuers to find the trapped men, to get them out safely. Praying as she'd never prayed before.

"You will, dear," Eleanor whispered, moving closer and enfolding her daughter in a hard hug. "If not, you'll deal with that then. Don't go there now."

"I've ruined everything."

"Oh, sweetheart. Life goes on, even after a disaster."

Julia stared at her mother, unable to hide her surprise.

"Don't look so shocked. Your father and I have been married a long time. It hasn't all been wine and roses."

"You never said anything."

Eleanor's eyes grew distant and her smile bittersweet. "You don't share the hard times with your children, not if you can help it. We've always protected you."

Julia had to agree with that. Her parents had been the ultimate barrier between her and the world.

"I don't know what to do, Mom." She had no idea what to do. Not now. Not if Linc—she swallowed the hurt—if Linc died. And if he lived? If he came out of that mine in one piece? What was she supposed to do then? She wasn't sure what she dreaded most.

Burying him or watching him walk away.

"Don't decide now. You're too upset. Take all the time you need." Eleanor pulled away as if sensing Julia needed space right now. "Don't let anyone tell you what you need. Not even me."

Julia hugged her mother. "Thanks, Mom."

Eleanor pushed a strand of hair out of Julia's eyes. "I love you, sweetheart. Stay here if you like. Breathe a little. I'll go check on your father."

Julia watched her mother walk back into the tent, recognizing her for the first time as a woman struggling to stay strong for someone she loved. *For me,* she thought and let herself smile a bittersweet smile.

The sound of footsteps, heavy with muck, kept Julia from thinking too hard. One shift must be leaving the mine. She turned to see a small group of men heading toward her.

Their faces were grimy as were the hard hats that were perched at odd angles on their heads, as if they'd pushed at them in frustration. The yellow slickers they wore were streaked with the black coal dust and their shoes caked with the mud they waded through.

Julia's heart skipped a beat. The first man in the group looked at her then, their gazes clashing. She recognized him, but couldn't have said from where.

Guiltily, she searched her battered memory and found no name.

"Mrs. Holmes?" The man's voice shook as he stopped a few feet away from her. "Is that Holmes down there your husband?"

The voice. She'd never forget Randy Watson again. He and his family lived down the street.

She looked up at the boy who'd become a man in such a short time and her tears blurred her vision. "Randy. I…I thought you were at college."

"I was, for a semester. Then we just couldn't afford the tuition. I came home at Christmas."

The few times they'd met in the neighborhood, she'd got the impression that he was a cutup with a quick mind and even faster reflexes with the comebacks.

He rushed closer while the rest of the crew continued down the hill. "I'm still taking classes. I'm not giving up," he reassured her.

She had to smile. He sounded more like the kid she remembered, rather than the man who now stood before her. "Good. Good." She didn't know what else to say. He didn't either. The silence stretched out between them.

"We're doing everything we can in there," he whispered, catching her gaze. He looked down at his hands, spreading them, palms up, between them. "I was using my hands even. Anything to get that rock out of the way."

Her heart hurt for him.

For them all.

"It's okay, Randy." She reached out to touch his arm, not caring if she got black grime on her hands.

"No, it's not." His words came out angry and she knew the anger wasn't at her, but at himself, at this whole mess. "Ryan's down there, too. I suppose you know that?"

"And Mike. Yeah."

"It's killing Missy."

"Missy?"

"My sister." He hunched his shoulders. "She and Ryan had a thing going. Then they had a fight just before he started working here."

"It's not her fault." Julia clearly recalled the conversation with Missy Watson after school last week. How long ago that seemed. She'd forgotten Randy and Missy were related. The girl was as pretty as Randy was handsome, with just enough sass to get her into trouble on a fairly regular basis. She could see what attracted Ryan to her.

"She won't believe that. Mom and Dad keep trying to tell her. They're worried about her. If this doesn't work out…"

She understood the girl's pain all too well.

"She won't leave her room."

"Do you think she'd come up here? Be with the rest of us?" Julia couldn't help but recall the comfort that Mamie and Rita had been for her. These women could help Missy, as well. She was too young to be facing this, much less carrying unnecessary guilt.

"I…" He shifted back and forth. "That'd be awfully nice for her, I think."

"Bring her up here if she'll come. She's welcome."

The eyes that turned to hers were boyish, young and afraid. She saw the damp shine in the fading light.

She'd started out comforting the boy and wasn't sure when the man had started comforting her. For a bit, just a little bit, she let her tears escape.

The loud, open-throttled roar of a motorcycle cut through the canyon and the tender moment was gone. With a solemn goodbye, Randy hastily wiped his eyes and followed his crew.

Julia watched him go, and let her gaze drift to beyond the fence. She could see the TV vans and the reporters mingling nearby. Two police cars sat angled across the road. Hank stood at the apex of the bumpers, not quite at attention, but straight and alert. His arms were behind his back, giving him a no-nonsense stance.

The motorcycle she'd heard rumbled up to him and stopped. The rider kicked the stand, killed the engine and sat back in the seat.

Slowly the man pulled the dark helmet from his head. Julia gasped. *Linc.* She took a step forward. Then the man's long brown hair fell to his shoulders. She froze in place.

It couldn't be.

Jace?

The last time she'd seen Linc's brother, they'd both been kids. How long ago it seemed. Linc didn't talk about Jace, never discussed the younger brother who'd run away from home and hadn't been heard from since. Until now, it seemed.

Hank shook Jace's hand, then after a brief discussion,

he directed Jace to park the big bike in the lot behind the fence. Julia didn't move, just watched him.

It was eerily like watching Linc move. She saw the same shape of his shoulders, the same tilt of his head, the same easygoing slouch. When he climbed off the bike, Jace awkwardly struggled to move on the uneven ground, as if he'd had some kind of injury or had sat too long. Maybe both.

He finished stowing the helmet and turned around to see her standing there, watching him. He walked slowly toward her. "Hello."

"Hi." The one word was a struggle. She tried again. "You're Jace, right?"

He frowned and the look in his eyes grew wary. "Jace Holmes." He tentatively offered his hand. "Do I know you? You look familiar."

"Julia Holmes. Used to be Alton. You probably don't remember me. I'm your sister-in-law."

His shock was strong and the expression on his face almost made her laugh. "Linc's married?"

"Yeah. Seven years now." She silently prayed that they'd at least get the chance at eight. "Welcome," she whispered.

"Shouldn't have taken this to get me here, I guess." He shifted from foot to foot. "But I had to come."

"Linc will be pleased."

"I don't know about that." Their eyes met. Linc might never even know Jace had arrived.

CHAPTER ELEVEN

Friday Afternoon, Twenty-Nine Hours Underground

How LONG COULD HE stay out here? Linc sank down onto a crate that had managed to survive the cave-in. The stone wall was rough but solid behind him. Out here, he left his light on, chasing away the heavy darkness.

He touched the screen on his watch. It glowed bright blue. Another two minutes had passed.

He glanced back at the canvas curtain. The shelter was their best hope of surviving until the rescuers reached them. It was one of the techniques he taught in safety classes.

He nearly scoffed at that. Safety classes. Lot of good they did now. New regulations had been enacted after the Sago disaster, but mines had years to comply. One lone man of the thirteen miners trapped in that West Virginia mine had survived to be rescued in 2006. Not only had there been numerous safety violations that led up to the explosion, but the communication about the rescue had been a mess. They'd even reported that the miners were all alive, only to have to tell the families the opposite later on. Part of Linc's job as an inspector was to see how well the properties were doing in getting prepared.

He wasn't impressed. Only problem was, who was he going to tell now?

He looked back at the shelter and cringed. He should get back. But just the thought made the walls seem to close in. The oxygen vanished in the small space. In there, he grew larger and felt sure everything would crush him.

Out here—even though it was a closed chamber—at least he could imagine a greater space. He could breathe without breaking into an anxious sweat.

It had been years since he'd experienced these panic attacks, since the nightmares of his father's burial. Closing his eyes, Linc tried to imagine himself someplace else, anywhere else that would take this feeling away.

The timer on his watch beeped. Shaking himself out of his misery, he picked up the hammer again and hit the pipe. He didn't expect a reply. They were more than two hundred feet beneath the surface. But he caught himself listening, waiting for an answering peal.

All he heard were footsteps approaching. He looked up to see Zach coming out of the shelter. It was the first time he'd seen him leave Casey's side since the accident.

"How are they doing?" Linc asked, referring to Casey and Gabe.

Zach shook his head. "They both need a doctor. But considering… Hell, at least Casey's still alive." Zach came over to where Linc sat and thumped down on the other side of the crate. "How're you doing, Inspector?" Zach tried to smile. "Robert's a jerk, you know. Don't let him get to you."

"He's just like my dad was." Linc shook his head. "He believes in what he's doing." He didn't like defending the man, but knew it was the truth.

"Hey, you got any paper in that pack of yours?"

"Uh, yeah. Why?" Linc leaned down and unzipped the backpack. He pulled out a legal pad that looked as if it had been run over by a truck, which, he realized, it might as well have been, a couple of times. The paper crinkled loudly as he handed it over.

"I thought that maybe I should write a note. You know, just in case, they, uh, don't reach us in time."

Linc couldn't respond, realizing that it hadn't even occurred to him to leave a note. What the hell would he write?

Zach took the paper and looked at Linc expectantly. Linc stared back. "Are you expecting me to write it in my own blood? Got a pencil in there?" Linc might have taken offense if the laughter hadn't sparked in Zach's eyes.

"Maybe I got a crayon or something," Linc teased back. He handed Zach a mechanical pencil.

"You're all right, Inspector." Zach bent over the notepad and started scribbling. The words came out quick at first, then slowed down as the initial rush faded. Zach looked up with a sigh. "You married, Inspector?"

"Yeah," he said aloud. *Sort of,* he added mentally.

"She's probably up there with my Trisha. Want me to add a message for her, or are you going to write your own note?"

"I don't know." Linc thought about it for a minute.

Should he write a note? What should he say? What shouldn't he say?

"You should, you know." Zach glanced at him. "My Trish at least deserves that much."

"Why? You got a confession to make?"

Zach chuckled. "No. Trish knows I'm faithful to her. She puts up with all kinds of crap. That's why I need to give her something positive to end on. I ain't been the best husband."

Somehow that didn't surprise Linc. He liked Zach, but he seemed like a man who knew how to party.

"Hey, if you make it good enough, maybe they'll put it in the paper like they did with that letter from Sago." Zach laughed again, but this time there was a note of sadness in his voice. That letter had been from one of the men who hadn't survived. His family had wanted to share his last words with the world. Reality could only be kept at bay for so long.

Linc knew about the Sago notes. He also knew that the men of Quecreek, who'd survived, had buried their notes, hiding them forever. They hadn't destroyed them though....

His father hadn't had the time to even think about a note. Maybe if he had, his mother would have had the closure she'd needed. Maybe she'd have been able to go on with her life instead of letting her grief destroy her.

Linc reached into the pack and pulled out another sheet of paper. This one was even more crumpled than the other. It was partially used. He'd started a list of things he wanted to keep when he and Julia sat down to divvy up their belongings.

The pen he pulled out was the red one he used to mark violations on the check-off sheet he had to turn in after each inspection. Slowly, carefully, he crossed out the list, negating his wishes.

He moved down to a blank line and wrote her name. *Julia.* He stopped, not sure what else to write, just staring at her name. How many times had he written that name and never really appreciated it?

He wanted to stay angry with her, he didn't want to think about how much he missed her, how empty the house was without her. Julia hadn't taken much when she'd left. She'd only packed a single overnight bag... but the house had lost something.

He didn't even begin to know how to say any of that. But he had to. Somehow...

Linc stared at the mutilated page, his mind empty of words and full of images. How, he asked himself, could he put a lifetime of feelings and thoughts onto a single sheet of paper?

A note that she'd read only if he died.

He struggled with the words, knowing they weren't enough. Never would be. The few meager words he managed to write swam as his eyes filled. Nothing made sense.

He thought of the junk drawer by the back door in the kitchen. Zach's comment about not being a good husband came to mind. Linc looked over at the other man. He wasn't writing, just staring at his own half-written page.

Linc turned away, hoping he didn't look as dejected as Zach. His mind returned to that drawer. Julia had been nagging him for months to get rid of all of his junk in it. All the stuff he never really used, but never threw away, either.

He could close his eyes and see the odd bits of shoelaces, paper clips and rubber bands. But there were useful things, too. Like the flathead screwdriver that he used to tighten the screws on the outside light that kept threatening to fall off the back of the house. Or the fishing hooks he was determined to use…if he ever got back up to the lake again.

Recently, though…she'd stopped nagging him about the drawer. He'd known things weren't right, but the fact that Julia didn't care about the mess anymore spoke volumes. She'd reached a point where she just didn't care, he realized, and that scared him.

There were so many questions he wanted to ask her, but he would hear no answers if she were reading this.

He tried to puzzle out what to say, but nothing came to him. Nothing but memories of joy and pain. He closed his eyes, wishing they'd go away, but they didn't. They only grew stronger, clearer.

Then it dawned on him why he couldn't write the note. It wasn't a goodbye he needed to leave Julia. He needed to find a way to fix all the hurt he'd put in her life, in her heart. And he just couldn't do that for her.

"Go to hell," she'd said last week. He nearly laughed. Maybe she was getting her wish after all.

Frustration ripped through him, and he nearly ripped the page in half, but he couldn't do it. Instead, he folded it and slipped it and the pen into his pocket. He needed to think about it, and they had some time left, he was sure.

"I'm going back in," he told Zach.

"Right behind you." Zach, too, folded his page and stuck it in his pocket. He held the pencil as if unsure what to do with it.

"Keep it. Maybe literary brilliance will strike."

Both men smiled. Linc led the way and they stepped through the canvas barrier to where the others were nothing but shadows against the eternal night. He settled back against the wall with a heavy sigh, trying to shut out the image of that old kitchen drawer and failing miserably.

Just let me out of here. I'll clean every damned drawer in the house if she wants.

Friday Night, 11:00 p.m.

WHENEVER PATRICK KELLY or other miners came to the tent, the scattered family groups gathered together. This time, as well. When the ragtag group of miners pulled open the tent flap, Julia sensed her parents shift beside her. Even Jace moved closer. Linc's brother had kept his distance, as if not quite sure where he fit in. She really couldn't blame him. He'd been gone too long.

Randy Watson looked around the room until he found her. Their eyes met and he quickly looked away. The small group of men parted, revealing his sister, Missy. The men had been protecting her, buffering her from the media outside, wrapping her in a cocoon.

The girl's eyes were puffy and red as if she'd cried for days and still had buckets of tears dammed up inside.

Julia stood and moved toward Missy. "Oh, sweetie,"

she said softly and opened her arms. Randy stepped aside and Missy ran into Julia's embrace, her sobs hard and painful.

Julia wanted to cry with her, but if she did, the flood would begin. She knew if she looked around that her mother, Mamie, Tricia, Rita, maybe even Shirley, would be holding back tears. Even the men, as tough as they all tried to be, were emotional at this point.

Julia recalled how Mamie had comforted her and held her, despite her own pain. She wanted to be that for Missy.

Julia pulled back, hoping to nudge the girl, and herself, into a calmer state. "Welcome." She looked up at Randy, realizing that the anguish on his face was at leaving his sister. "I'll take care of her, Randy. You do what you need to do."

He nodded and turned to leave.

"Randy?" Missy called. "Thanks. And be careful."

He smiled at her, and Julia added her own well wishes.

And then the men were gone. Back to the work of getting them all out of this horrid situation. Julia kept her arm around Missy and guided her to where she and her family had set up a small group of chairs. It had become her little corner of the tent, and she wanted Missy to have a place where she felt safe and welcome.

She saw a bit of herself in the girl. She knew what it was like to love someone so much that the possibility they might not always be there was unthinkable. Instead of falling into her own despair, she focused on making Missy feel comfortable.

The tent—and these circumstances—were miles and years away from the classroom where they normally saw each other. Julia swallowed, realizing that world might never be as it had been again.

"I'm here for you." Julia spoke softly, carefully, laying a hand on Missy's arm.

She looked across the tent at Jack Sinclair. How long ago and how inconsequential the school board and the anger he'd thrown at her seemed. "Everyone's doing their best to save our guys." Julia tried to reassure everyone.

The sound of Mamie's metal walker broke into their conversation. Julia looked around and was gratified that the others had come closer, their hearts going out to the girl who was obviously falling to pieces in front of them.

Rita stepped forward and, as Julia had done, she slipped an arm around Missy. "Ryan's going to be awfully happy that you're here."

"I didn't know if he was still interested." Missy hedged as only a teenage girl, lovesick and afraid, could hedge.

"Oh, he's interested." Rita tried to smile through her own worry.

Missy visibly perked up and for the first time since Randy had brought her into the tent, she looked around without weeping.

"You did a good thing, my dear." Mamie's curled hand settled on Julia's shoulder. She glanced up to see the old woman smiling at her.

In that moment, Julia felt the bond that only other

women would understand. The feeling known since time immemorial by all the wives, lovers and mothers who had watched their men go off to work, or to war or to any other dangerous pursuit. Women left behind to wait, worry and tend. The women who surrounded her now were her comrades in arms and she appreciated them for being that.

Shuffling feet created a stir at the tent opening and Patrick Kelly strode in. He was alone this time, which was unusual. No team of engineers flanked and protected him. In his hand, he carried a long roll of paper.

He waved at Jack Sinclair and Julia's father, Raymond. "Can you help me, guys?" Since he hadn't brought reinforcements, he made do with what he had.

Together, the men unrolled a large map. Dark lines, cross marks and circles had been drawn on it in black marker. A large box took up one corner.

The families closed in around him and the trapped-rabbit look returned to his eyes, but he swallowed and continued. "Okay, folks. I've brought this so I can walk you through what we're doing."

Everyone groaned. They were so tired of technical explanations. It was time for answers. Julia ground her teeth in frustration, but still, she moved closer, wanting something she could understand.

"This is the geological survey of the mountain," Patrick began. "These two Xs are where we're drilling first. This one is for air. This one, a little to the north, is bigger. We'll send the equipment, cameras and communication devices down this one." He pointed to the first mark.

Jack and Raymond nodded. They understood and weren't reacting with any alarm. Julia felt Missy slip her hand in hers, her fingers stiff and cold.

Mamie hobbled forward. "How far down have they gotten?" The clatter of her walker accented each word.

Patrick sighed and turned away from the map. "Fifty feet."

"Fifty feet?" Julia cried. "You said the men are at least two hundred feet down."

"At least," Patrick agreed. "But so far, it's all we've got."

"When do you expect to reach them?" Jace's voice was calm and deep, so unlike Julia's shrill demand.

"Tomorrow morning at the earliest," Patrick said softly and Julia almost fell to her knees. "The big drill's being set up now. We'll start that as soon as it's ready."

"Hey," a man called from outside the tent. "Hey." Before any of them could move, Randy Watson shoved his head through the opening, his smile wide. He didn't wait for an invitation to speak. "We got taps."

The room erupted with noise. Hugs were everywhere. Julia neither knew nor cared whose arms were around her or who she held. She just knew hope was alive and well.

"How many?" Patrick's smile, while genuine, was tempered.

"Seven. All seven alive."

Friday Night, Thirty-Three Hours Underground

LINC SETTLED BACK IN the shelter, this time right next to the canvas, near the opening that eased his claustrophobia. He pulled out the note, glaring at it. Maybe he shouldn't have even started to write it.

His heart hurt just to think about it. Closing his eyes, he leaned his head against the wall. He tried to picture Julia reading it, hoping to find a clue to what to write, what words might give her peace. But each time he envisioned her reading it, he saw the tears, the pain on her face, and heard her sobs.

Because while he knew their marriage was on shaky ground, he truly believed she still loved him. He knew he still loved her, so why couldn't they find that simple truth when they were together?

Why did the angry words stop them from reaching for each other? Why did the hurt not allow for the needed comforting hug? Hell, why didn't the passion he knew they shared not overcome the hesitancy?

"Your thoughts are too loud," Gabe whispered and his chuckle disintegrated into a cough. Linc helped him sit up better and the cough subsided.

"What's that supposed to mean, old man?"

"You're thinking too hard. Trying to fix all the world's troubles…or at least those you think you're leaving behind."

"Hardly. I can't even fix my own, much less the world's."

Gabe laughed again, but no coughing fit followed,

thank goodness. "Zach convince you to write that good-bye letter?"

This time Linc chuckled. "Thinking about it."

"Thinking don't get it done."

That was true. "You writing one?"

"Nope. Don't have to."

"Why?"

"Wrote one years ago—when I had my first heart attack. Left it in the safe deposit box. Shirley'll find it when I'm gone one day."

"What'd you say? How did you say goodbye?"

"I didn't. I told her how much I appreciated having her, not how much I'd hate it without her. Think positive. Leave your wife with a light to see through the darkness ahead. Don't extinguish it by pointing out what's hurting her."

Linc stared at the older man. "How'd you get so wise down here in the bowels of the earth?"

"Maybe talking to God near the devil's playground gives you points." Gabe whispered the words, and Linc knew he'd drifted off to sleep, his energy spent trying to comfort someone else.

Linc let Gabe's words soak in. Maybe he'd gather a few points of his own. Closing his eyes, he wondered if he even remembered how to pray.

CHAPTER TWELVE

Saturday Morning, 3:00 a.m.

"WHY THE HELL IS LINC working in the mines?"

Jace spoke intently, yet so softly that Julia thought she might have imagined it. "I thought after what happened to Dad, he'd never go underground."

"He's not a miner, he's an inspector." There was no reason to believe Jace had any idea what Linc actually did for a living. "He only spends part of his time underground."

Julia stared at Jace. The man was nothing like she'd thought the boy would become. He was rough and worn. His anger lived in his eyes, and she wasn't sure there was anything else behind that anger.

"You're Fancy Pants."

She thought the curving of his lips might be a smile. The sound that came from his throat wasn't quite a laugh—more of a cackle if men did that. "I hated that nickname in school. Your brother gave it to me."

"I know. And he was damned proud of it at the time, if I remember."

"Thanks." She let her sarcasm show. "Try to forget that, would you?"

"No." He paused and the pseudo smile vanished. He hid behind his coffee cup for an instant.

Julia wondered what was going on inside his mind. She almost feared his next words, and she knew there were more.

"I don't have that many good memories of growing up. I'll keep that one, thanks," he finally said.

The silence stretched out long and heavy. She wanted to tell him to keep talking. She didn't want her mind to fill with the images of Linc and the others still trapped, waiting...hoping...dying.

"Where have you been for the past ten years?" she ventured.

"On the road." He fell silent again. "I left home and ended up in Sturgis, South Dakota, and I've been on the move ever since."

She'd heard of the rough motorcycle town and stared at him. "You were only sixteen when you left." She recalled news stories of brawls, gang fights and drugs there. It was no place for a kid.

"Yeah, and I grew up real fast," he whispered.

"How did you survive?"

His eyes grew distant. "I almost didn't."

This time she knew he wouldn't elaborate. She didn't push. She didn't want to know. Silently, she prayed that Jace wouldn't share any of those memories with Linc, if he survived to hear him. Linc's guilt over his brother running away was already too strong.

"I finally landed in L.A. That's where I met Mac. He's the only reason I'm alive today."

Julia heard the reverence, the emotion in Jace's voice.

She wanted to thank the man but got the impression he wasn't around to thank. "Jace?"

She spoke to call him back to the present, knowing he was far away. "I know Linc will want to know what the past ten years have been like, but—" How did she ask him to lie, to sugarcoat the truth? "He feels responsible for your leaving, for all the pain in your life." There, she'd said it.

He turned to glare at her then. "You're kidding, right?"

She refused to squirm under the intensity of his stare, but it wasn't easy.

"What are you most afraid of...him feeling more guilty, or him gloating over how he managed to make something of his life instead of ending up a street rat?" he asked.

"No, that's not what I meant."

"Why are you trying to protect him?"

"I'm not."

"Yes, you are. He's a grown man. He was an adult when I left. I won't lie to him. I owe him the truth."

She wanted to argue, but the look on his face, the hard determination there, stopped her. "I—" The words stuck in her throat. She tried again. "The last couple of years, losing your mom, losing—" She swallowed hard. "It's been hard."

"Life's hard, Fancy Pants."

"Stop it." She turned to walk away, and was surprised when his hand closed around her arm.

"Answer me one thing," he said in her ear. "Why are *you* here? You left him. I heard your folks talking. You were moving out of the house when the call came. What do you care what happens to him?"

"He's my husband."

"And I repeat, you're leaving him." He nearly spat the words. "Prove him right, why don't you."

"What does that mean?"

"You've been married to him how long? I've been gone ten years and I still know him better than you do. He's never felt good enough for you. He's always known he'd never live up to your expectations."

"That's ridiculous. He's successful. He's fine."

"He let you go." Jace released her arm. "He didn't even come after you when you left, did he?"

"No." The single word tore from Julia's throat. He *hadn't* come after her. He'd let her go. He'd stayed on the front porch while she'd packed, while she drove away. He'd stayed in the house, their home, making a mess of it. He'd never tried to reach her. It wasn't true. He couldn't possibly feel inadequate.

And yet he hadn't come after her.

He'd let her go.

Her vision blurred, and she glanced away from Jace, the only person who had the nerve to tell her what she needed to know. Even Linc hadn't told her the truth.

Jace nodded and after an unnerving, accusatory glare, he headed for the coffee. She watched him go, wondering why she'd thought he was Linc at first. Other than the physical resemblance, they were nothing alike— were they?

She was willing to give Linc's brother the benefit of the doubt for his mood. These weren't normal circumstances, but if he was that worried about his brother, why hadn't he contacted him even once in the past ten years? Why hadn't he bothered to call when his mother died? Linc would have appreciated that.

While Linc could slip into that same moody, angry place, he did it infrequently. She remembered how he'd allowed his emotions to rule him in high school, but he'd grown up, managed to find an even balance. He seldom gave in to his emotions.

The last time…

The last time had nearly destroyed them both.

Only once in their entire marriage did Julia remember having Linc all to herself. He was always so busy, taking care of the house, his mother until her death, his job—all things she appreciated. All that made her love him.

And they were all things that took him away from her more than they brought him to her.

He always tried to do the best for everyone else.

After she'd lost the baby, he'd taken time off from everything.

He'd packed her up and driven out to the mountains, to a quaint cabin on a small lake. He'd rented it for a whole week.

Why hadn't they even talked about doing something like that again? Why had they let life separate them?

Why had *she* let things come between them?

Slowly, because her mind reluctantly accepted it, she realized she'd pushed him away. Looking around the room, she realized she'd pushed everyone away. Her parents. Her neighbors. People who could have been her friends. But mostly, Linc.

All because she was afraid to face her past and risk being hurt. Instead, she'd nearly lost them completely.

Saturday Morning, Thirty-Seven Hours Underground

LINC KNEW THAT SOMEWHERE, up on the surface, teams were scrambling to dig through the tons of rock between them and the outside world.

He knew the procedures. The plans that would be put into action. He wasn't sure if the knowledge was a blessing or a curse.

Linc had only met Halston, the mine's CEO, once, but he'd worked with the Director of the Mining Commission many times. He liked and respected Patrick Kelly. The man knew his business. He'd been underground for years, knew the earth and its quirks as well as any miner.

Knowing that Patrick was in charge of this rescue operation alleviated some of Linc's stress.

If only he could rid himself of the anxiety of being trapped. Of this horrid fear that threatened to eat his sanity.

"Dear Heavenly Father." Ryan's whisper was deep with pain and shaky with fear. Linc knew he shouldn't listen, knew that he should leave the boy to his confession. But the words were too real to be ignored.

"Forgive me for all the trouble I've been to Mom and Dad. And for all the bad things I've thought, you know, about Missy." His voiced trailed off. "And for hurting Mrs. Holmes."

Linc started. How had Ryan hurt Julia? The kid hadn't done much except decide to quit school, but from Ryan's point of view, the whole mess probably seemed worse than it was.

"I suppose you heard that." Ryan was addressing him now.

"Yeah," Linc admitted.

"Sorry. I really didn't mean to cause trouble between you and her."

Linc turned to stare in the direction of the boy's voice. The darkness was too thick to see anything at this point.

"What do you mean?" He wanted to hear what Ryan had to say, but he had no intention of admitting that trouble between him and Julia went back way longer than this issue.

"I heard her talking to Ms. Daily, the teacher she's subbing for—you know, the one who's out on maternity leave?"

Yeah, yeah, get on with it, Linc wanted to say, but wisely held back. "About me?" he asked instead. He was shocked that Julia had said anything to the other teacher—she seldom confided in anyone, even him. If she was reaching out to a stranger, she must have felt more alone than he'd ever guessed. He wanted to know what she'd talked about.

"Not exactly."

"Then what?"

"About her teaching job. Something about how she thought moving to the high school would help."

"Help?" Linc was starting to feel like a parrot, but couldn't stop himself.

"I don't really know any details. She mentioned something about babies."

The air stabbed Linc's lungs as he gasped. He'd been so stupid. He'd thought that if they just ignored it and went on with their lives, they'd both eventually get over their traumatic loss. That was why he'd shrugged off Julia's desire to see a fertility specialist. If they didn't acknowledge the problem, they could move on. Obviously, she hadn't. She'd quit the job she loved, taking herself away from the pain of seeing the children that would never be hers.

He closed his eyes, the visions behind his lids clear, familiar and all too painful.

Julia, her belly rounded with their child. The nursery she'd worked so hard to decorate. Her empty arms and vacant stare when he'd brought her home that wretched day.

And he saw her now, worry and pain on her face. Tears on her cheeks and fear in her heart. He knew her. Knew that though she'd hide it, her emotions would overwhelm her. Watching her pain had been worse than feeling his own. He'd promised her—and himself—that he'd never put her through that again.

He'd broken that promise.

Zach came over and sat beside them. "You know what's going on up there." It was a statement.

"I have a pretty good idea."

"So, is Gabe being straight? Is there really a drill that can get us the hell out of here?" Zach asked.

Linc waited a beat, noting the worry on the other man's face. "Yeah, there is. Remember Quecreek?"

"The one where they made the big drill?"

"Yeah." That rescue was famous in the industry—the only one in decades where everyone survived. Hundreds of people had worked round the clock on that one.

"Think they'll bring it in for us?" Zach sounded almost as if he thought they might not bother.

"It's most likely already here."

Zach nodded again, his shoulders visibly relaxing, accepting the information. "And how will they know where to drill?"

"The air and communication holes are tests."

Zach stared up at the ceiling, as if listening to the distant grinding that had become constant background noise. "You think they'll be better than Utah?" Both men paused, avoiding each other's gaze.

"They'd better be," Linc whispered. "There were never any signals in Utah. They never heard a thing." They'd never even found the bodies of the men who'd died in that disaster back in 2007.

Zach sat a minute longer, then, just as they all had done numerous times before, he picked up the ball-peen hammer and slammed it against the pipe. The bangs were as much a message as a release of emotion. Linc worried that the pipe might shatter.

It didn't. The seven peals for seven alive rang loud enough to haunt Linc's nightmares in years to come.

God, he wanted those years.

Saturday Morning, 5:00 a.m.

JACE STARTLED JULIA WHEN he sat back down on the chair, the steaming cup of coffee nestled in his hands. He stared down into the drink as if there were some magical answer there.

"I should have gone home to see Mom."

"Why didn't you?"

He met her gaze then and the awful pain in his eyes sliced clear through her.

"I was too busy with my buddy, Jack Daniel's." He looked down again, but she didn't catch more than a faint flicker of emotion. "I keep track of things online when I can get to a connection. By the time I'd sobered up, the services were already over."

"Even so, Linc would have liked to hear from you."

"Yeah." The way he drew out the word told her he didn't believe her.

"You don't know Linc now." She felt anger growing toward this man who had caused so much pain to so many. "I know you thought he was an adult when you left, but he was only twenty-one."

His temper, swift and sharp, surfaced and died just as quickly. "I didn't make the best choices then, and I don't always make them now." He stood and took a sip of coffee as if preparing his thoughts. "I only knew about Linc because I stopped for a drink and saw his picture on some update on the television over the bar." The self-loathing was strong in his voice. "The only reason I'm here…"

He didn't finish his sentence.

"Is to see if he's dead?" she finished for him. Just saying it hurt.

"Yes and no."

She stood impatiently. "What do you want, Jace? Money? Absolution? Information? I can't give you any of that."

"I don't want a damned thing from you." He turned away. He tossed the coffee cup into a nearby trash can, the contents splashing over the rim. "You're not why I'm here, so get over yourself."

"That's enough." Shirley stepped forward, surprising them both. "This isn't the time or place to rehash the past. We've got enough going on."

Jace glared at them both and left the tent. Julia looked over at Shirley. "Thank you," she whispered.

"You're welcome," Shirley said without any warmth or feeling. "But I didn't do it for you." She turned and walked away.

Julia stared after both of them, drained and fed up with being here, with all these people, with all this noise, with everything and everyone.

She just wanted it to be over.

But she feared the outcome too much to make it a true prayer.

CHAPTER THIRTEEN

Saturday Morning, Thirty-Nine Hours Underground

LINC KNEW, AS THEY ALL DID, that time was running out. Even with the drills overhead, it was hard to keep up their spirits.

"Hey, Casey," Zach said. The sound of his voice surprised the others. The desperation in it didn't. "Next weekend's that fishing competition up at Trout Lake. I'm game if you are."

Casey only grunted an answer, but for some reason it was enough. Linc, and, he hoped, everyone else, took reassurance from the fact that Casey was still with them.

Hopefully heading to Trout Lake next weekend.

Trout Lake. Linc knew the men were trying to find memories to distract themselves. Positive things to think about. Good thoughts to go out on.

Linc didn't have to work at it. There were no stronger memories for him than that lake. With Julia.

The week at the cabin with her felt like a lifetime ago. Earlier, he'd avoided thinking about it, but now with the end so close, he had to face it, had to go anywhere but here.

He'd been a different person then, which, looking

back, probably wasn't a good thing. That guy had been alive and caring. The changes in both him and Julia had been gradual. Had either of them even really noticed? He realized that the wedge between them had begun sometime after they returned from the lake.

He recalled that first night as one of the highlights, albeit a bittersweet one, of their life together. He let his mind go there, let his memories comfort him.

He'd lain beside her, listening to her sleep. That was why he'd taken her to the cabin—sleep was what she desperately needed—and yet his heart and body hadn't cooperated. They wanted more. So much more.

Maybe it was the quiet in the mine, or the desperate situation, or just being away from Julia, but the grief he'd locked away suddenly sprang loose.

Julia had wanted a baby as long as he could recall, but until the tiny life became reality, he'd felt disconnected from it all. They'd celebrated the coming child as couples do, but the difference in his life was minimal. It was *her* body experiencing the changes.

And then came that awful day. Julia had been in the nursery, putting up the duck-and-kitten wallpaper border she'd spent days searching for, when the first pain had hit.

He'd rushed her to the hospital, all the time feeling so inept. He'd never get over the sense that he should have been able to do something to help her, to help *them*. It was that same sense of helplessness he'd felt when his father had been trapped. His inability to take care of the people he loved made him feel inadequate.

The doctors had fought to save the baby—his son—but in the end, they'd failed.

And he'd nearly lost Julia, too.

Linc didn't know when the tears came or when he fell asleep. He let his mind escape. Then suddenly she was with him and they were at the cabin. Together.

Sleep-mussed, alive and incredibly beautiful, sipping at his leftover whiskey, she looked at him with a desire in her eyes that eclipsed his own.

The firelight was dim, but it provided enough illumination that he could see her clearly—very clearly. His Julia was as beautiful as ever.

He knew her. Knew so much about her. The feel of her soft skin. The taste of her kisses. The sound of her sweet cries of fulfillment. What it felt like to be inside her.

Linc stood, half-afraid that if he sat so close to her much longer, watching her, needing her, he'd do what he'd sworn he wouldn't.

This week was about her, about her recovery. That may or may not include making love, but it would be her choice. Her decision.

Not his, and most certainly not at the level of intensity his body was asking for. He ran a hand through his hair. Maybe he should go for a run around the lake. He had to relieve this pounding need somehow.

She stopped him, pressing up against him, her body hot against his. She stood on tiptoe and gently kissed each of his eyes.

Linc stifled a groan.

Did she have a clue what she was doing to him? She'd

always been the one to take the first step in their relationship. She'd had to dare him to kiss her. The night
she'd stomped across campus...

She'd led the way and he'd so very gladly followed.
Not because he didn't want her. But because he wanted
her too much and was scared of hurting her. Scared of
screwing up the best thing in his life.

But this time was different. He didn't know where
she was headed.

"So, you think you're ready?" His voice cracked.

"Oh, yeah." She gave the waistband of his pajamas
a hard tug and he smiled back.

"But not yet." He pulled her closer, if that were possible, and lowered his head to kiss all the way from her
ear to her collarbone. "Or we'll be finished before we
even get started. It's been too long."

"Way too long."

His lips devoured hers, and he couldn't seem to hold
her tight enough. He had no intention of ever letting
go.

Julia sighed in contentment, and Linc reveled in the
feel of her hands sliding down his spine, to his lower
back, over the waistband of the damned pajamas. What
had he been thinking when he'd packed them?

Not this.

He pulled back, wanting to see her face. The fireplace
flames reflected in her eyes, casting warmth through
her and to him. He trailed kisses over her eyes and her
cheeks.

Julia leaned back as well, pressing her hips tighter to
his, letting the light play over the slope of her breasts.

He moved lower, parting the loose robe. His lips closed over her nipple and his tongue danced over the pebbled tip.

She cried out and pressed her fingers against the nape of his neck, urging him on.

He was more than ready to oblige.

Her clothes fell away, scattering across the rug in a haphazard pattern. His robe and pajamas joined the mix and somehow they were stretched out in front of the hearth.

Their bodies bathed in the dancing firelight, they both looked their fill, something he hadn't done in a long time.

Every inch of her glowed. She was ready for him. Very ready, but Linc wanted this to last.

He moved slowly down her body, alternating kisses and licks to the shadows and valleys. Of her breasts. Of her waist. Of the marks that would always be a reminder of what her body had been through. Slowly, softly, reverently, he kissed each of the tiny lines.

Her fingers clung to him, at first running through his hair then curling and gripping his shoulders as her desire escalated.

"Linc. Please. Now."

"Patience," he whispered, though he had every intention of giving her what she wanted. His need matched hers. He wanted to fill her, to feel her around him as her tension built.

Unable to hold back, he thrust into her. He wanted to give, yet selfishly knew he'd relish the outcome as much as she did.

They moved together. The same rhythm, the same pace as they'd done for ages but different this time. Sweeter. Stronger. As if they were now even closer in tune.

He tried to hold back, to move carefully, but Julia matched his moves and urged him on. Clenching his teeth, he barely kept control, feeling her release building higher, tighter. And then it crested through her, and she cried his name. He was lost in her, fully and completely.

Moments passed as they returned to earth. The fire popped and Linc's mind clicked back into gear. His breath ragged, he lifted himself off her, leaning on his elbows to peer down into her eyes.

"Thank you," she whispered.

"For?" He gave her his best wry grin.

"For everything."

He kissed her then, softly, gently, and knew that he'd never been more afraid. He swallowed hard and buried his face against her neck. "Ah, babe. I'm sorry."

"What?"

He doubted she could have been more shocked if he'd dumped cold water on her. He knew he had to explain. They should have had this conversation before making love. "We didn't use any protection. You could get pregnant."

She stared at him. "And that's a bad thing because…?" She pushed, and he let her move away.

He grabbed her robe and handed it to her, then pulled on his own. "It's too soon. Besides, I'm not sure I can go through that again. I certainly don't expect you to."

"And you thought we would come up here for a whole week and not make love?"

"No. I brought stuff." He thought about the box of condoms at the bottom of his suitcase.

Julia yanked hard on her belt and stood. She picked up the whiskey glass and nearly took a drink. She stopped with the glass against her lips, as if she wasn't sure she could stop once she started, then crossed to the sink to dump it out. She took her time rinsing the glass before turning to face him.

"It's not your fault. Mine, neither. I need you, Linc. Don't you want me?"

He hesitated, knowing his answer would hurt her. "I'll always, *always* want you." He stepped closer to her, but didn't reach for her. The very thought of not wanting her was painful. "But I'm not sure we're ready for that yet."

It had taken three years for Julia to get pregnant once they'd decided to start a family. Even she had nearly given up. He couldn't watch that hope die again.

"Oh, Linc. I can't live afraid of what might happen. I'm more afraid of what we'll miss out on." She faced him and reached out to run her fingers along his jaw.

He flinched, not because he didn't want her touch, but because he did. Too much to resist.

Her voice was so quiet that he had to strain to hear her. "I want to have your baby."

"I know."

"A child would be a part of both of us. A part of you that I'd always have."

He found himself reaching for her again, agreeing to

keep trying. Agreeing to anything that would take the hurt away.

Linc jerked painfully awake. Julia's words echoed through time and the dark, cold mountain where he now sat huddled.

He hadn't kept that promise. Despite trashing the box of condoms, Julia hadn't gotten pregnant in the months since. She wanted to see a fertility doctor. That's why the distance grew between them, why the arguments began.

Linc truly believed that if they were meant to have a child, they would. Julia did *not* agree. Maybe he was avoiding reality, but so was she. Even a doctor couldn't guarantee everything would work out. Linc saw only the heartache waiting for them if they went down that path.

Now, sitting here in the chamber that would most likely become his grave, his emotions waffled back and forth. He was thankful he wasn't putting a child through what his father's ordeal had put him through. And yet... Julia so wanted a baby, and he'd failed her. He hadn't left her with that piece of himself she'd asked for. Linc's throat tightened up. This time Julia wouldn't be able to kiss the tears away.

Saturday Morning, 5:30 a.m.

ANGER, FRUSTRATION AND JUST plain stress all compelled Julia to follow Shirley. "What the hell do you mean you didn't do it for me?" She reached the woman's side and grabbed her arm. "You're not walking away from that kind of a comment."

"How *dare* you."

"How dare I what? Question you? Follow you? Try to understand what's going on?" Disgusted, Julia shook her head. "Give me a break. You don't care about anyone else's feelings, do you, Shirley? You just want everyone to be calm. Well, I *can't* be calm."

Julia glared at Shirley. Shirley made her feel uncomfortable and unwelcome, especially since she'd talked to Ryan about not going into the mine. The lasting effects of that hostility reached out now.

Julia stood her ground and realized all too quickly that every eye in the tent had turned toward them. There was no going back now. "Is it just Ryan or is there something else? I get the feeling your animosity has something to do with my husband's job," she added.

"You're damned right it does." Shirley leaned in close. "Since the accidents over the past couple of years, the government has become paranoid. The inspectors, like your husband, are too powerful."

Julia stared in shock. "So, you think it's okay for mine owners to get away with risking their employees' lives?"

"That's not what I said."

"It's what you meant and exactly what's happened for years."

"What do you know?"

"I know plenty." Julia felt the blood rushing through her body. Now she saw what Linc was up against every day. She didn't know how he kept doing it, but she was proud of him. "Does the name Alton Mining ring any bells?"

She refused to look at her father. She didn't have to wait for Shirley to answer. The color drained from the older woman's face. "I see it does. My father owned that mine."

Everyone in the industry had heard of the Alton Mine tragedy that had killed fifteen men and trapped ten others for two days. The accident had caused the creation of an entire system of mining regulation, the system that now required men like Linc.

"I know both sides of this industry. My husband does what he does because he believes in it. Because his father was one of the men who died."

Shirley's eyes shone but Julia didn't take time to consider why. She barely breathed, much less thought.

"Every mining law in this country is written with honest, innocent men's blood. Linc works to make sure that blood wasn't shed in vain." She stopped, the stricken look on Shirley's face telling her she'd gone too far. Her hand flew to cover her mouth as she became painfully aware of what she'd said.

Silence was the only answer for a long time.

Mamie stepped forward, leaning heavily on her walker. "Julia, you don't know."

"Don't know what?"

"It's no one's business," Shirley said.

Julia rounded on her again. "It sure is if it's why you treat me like a second-class citizen. We're all in this together, Shirley. Everyone is at risk of losing someone they love."

Shirley's face crumpled and suddenly Julia knew. Knew that she'd hit a nerve, knew that she'd discovered why Shirley was angry with her, and most important, she'd discovered the source of Shirley's greatest pain.

"Who did you lose?" Julia asked softly, as nonthreateningly as possible, her anger receding and allowing her to see the other woman's agony.

Shirley just sat staring at Julia. Her eyes filled with what seemed like long-held-in tears.

"It's time to let it out," Mamie said as softly as Julia had, adding the gentle touch of her hand on Shirley's shoulder.

Finally she spoke. "My son. Wayne." Shirley's voice trembled.

The tears spilled over, but Julia was impressed that Shirley sat up straighter and met Julia's eyes. And, for the first time, she didn't look defensive.

"He was nineteen. He'd been wanting to walk in his daddy's shoes since he was old enough to know what Gabe did. He wanted to be just like him, and he loved the idea of mining." She took a deep breath and paused to wipe her eyes. "Gabe kept trying to get him to think about going to college. When Wayne found out he could go into the mine at seventeen, we couldn't keep him in school. He worked at the Piney Ridge Mine for two years before the explosion. They say he didn't suffer, which I'm thankful for. But…" Her voice trailed off and her erect posture fell. Sobs filled the tent.

Julia was overwhelmed by sympathy for the other woman. She resisted the urge to wrap her arms around Shirley. She knew neither of them was ready for that.

Losing a child was never easy. No matter when it happened. Julia looked into Mamie's eyes where tears for Shirley and herself lurked. Rachel sat with her arms around her belly. Julia was sure she was promising herself she'd never let her child go into a mine. Shirley, however, provided a potent reminder that no matter how hard parents tried, they just couldn't control their kids or the world they lived in.

Julia's thoughts filled with the memory of her own lost baby. She doubted the pain would ever go away.

"It makes me so mad when you say we shouldn't let the kids go into the mine. Makes me feel like I failed as a mom." Shirley's anger came back full-force. It was what kept her going.

"I'm sorry it came across that way." Julia needed to make peace between them. "That's not how I meant it. You tried. You tried your hardest, I'm sure. But you couldn't accomplish it without help." Julia knew she was heading toward very shaky ground. "You needed help from the mines. They shouldn't let the kids in. That's what I was getting at."

Rita looked at Julia with grateful eyes and knew she was thinking of her sons—especially Ryan. They both faced Shirley, waiting for her reaction.

It came, but it wasn't what Julia expected. Shirley shifted in her seat. Scooting to the edge, she lifted her head and she glared at them through her tears. But Julia knew the anger wasn't for her.

"You're wrong," Shirley whispered and looked away. "I didn't try." She tilted her head toward the vacant podium that had become the symbol of the mine's management. "I thought the life would be good for him. I...I encouraged him."

There were murmurs of pain from all the women. And a heartbreaking echo from the men. Julia moved closer to the older woman and put her arm gently around her shoulders. Losing a child was the ultimate pain. Living with the belief you'd contributed to that loss would be nothing short of hell.

Looking up, Julia saw not only Jack Sinclair standing there, but her father. The regret in Raymond Alton's eyes was tempered by a glimmer of pride she hoped was for her.

Shirley crumbled then and Julia held on tight.

Patrick entered the tent at that moment and the air seemed to vanish from the room. No one moved as they met his bleak stare. He remained in the doorway, but despite the distance, his words couldn't have done more damage if he'd thrown a bomb into the middle of the room.

"The bit broke."

Saturday Morning, Thirty-Nine-and-a-Half Hours Underground

A LOUD BOOM VIBRATED through the mountain over-head. The men all ducked, raising their arms to cover their heads from falling rock. Had the tip of the drill broken through? Linc looked up but saw nothing, heard nothing but silence.

Inside the shelter where they all crouched, the silence

became a presence that cloaked them, like the black mine dust Linc could feel on his skin.

"What happened?" The kid spoke first, his voice quavering just a little.

No one wanted to say it, but they knew it wasn't good. Not good at all.

CHAPTER FOURTEEN

Saturday Morning, 6:30 a.m.

PATRICK'S WORDS TRIGGERED a landslide of silence. He must have said more because his lips kept moving, but Julia's brain was on overload and nothing made sense. He left and she turned toward the exit. She felt Shirley move away, disappearing into the crowd and her own pain. Julia's temples pounded and her neck ached. Nothing helped. She had aspirin in her purse, but knew it wouldn't react well with all the coffee she'd drunk.

They aren't going to make it. A scream bubbled up inside her. Her throat convulsed and she wrapped her arms around her middle, afraid she'd throw up. Breathing deeply, she hid her face in her hands, but she couldn't seem to make her lungs expand.

She felt the tentative touch of a hand on her shoulder. Missy was trying to comfort her, but she flinched away from the girl's touch.

"Sorry," Missy whispered and stepped back.

"No. Don't be." Julia fought for control. "I just don't know if I can take any more." She'd been trying to keep up a good front for everyone. So her parents wouldn't worry. To support Missy and the other women. But the tension from dealing with Shirley had left its mark.

The strength she'd been struggling so hard to shore up crumbled. She couldn't pretend anymore. Couldn't keep up the pretense that she was okay. She wasn't okay, not now and maybe never again.

She needed out. Out of here. Out of this whole mess. She didn't want to spend another minute here. She stood and hurried out of the tent, nearly at a run.

"Let her go," she heard Mamie tell someone. Bless her.

Julia ran down the hill, past the mine opening where the workers barely looked up. Dawn had just broken and the lamps from several of the men's hats were still on as they trudged from the hole.

She rounded the corner of the double-wide trailer that served as the mine office and halted in her tracks. There, at the edge of the dirt lot, sat Linc's truck. The navy blue and chrome shone in the early-morning sun.

The tangible evidence that he was here hurt and yet soothed her. She slowed her steps, approaching the big blue beast with trepidation.

Linc never locked his truck. Julia wasn't sure he even knew how. She pulled the door open and the stale car air from the days it had been sitting neglected washed over her. The familiar smell of the truck soothed her. Dirt. Grease. Vinyl. But no trace of the pine-tree air freshener she'd put in here months ago and that still hung from the rearview mirror.

Usually she hated the smell of the truck, but now it was as if Linc were here, nearby. She climbed up on the driver's side of the bench seat and let the familiar warmth surround her. She closed her eyes and pictured his face. She thought about the last time she'd seen him in the truck, but found that a painful memory. She'd been so mad at him that night. Instead, she opened her eyes and looked around.

The man was *not* a housekeeper by any stretch of the imagination. The far window had nose and drool marks from the stray terrier Linc had found and taken to the shelter a couple of weeks ago. Candy wrappers, soda cans and his toolbox sat on the floor of the passenger side.

He had left a windbreaker and his heavy leather jacket draped over the back of the seat. She reached for the jacket and slipped it on. Its warm weight and the faint spice of his aftershave brought tears to her eyes.

This place was so…so Linc. An ache formed in her chest, and she struggled against the hopes and dreams that now seemed lost. Curious, she leaned across the seat and opened the glove box.

Her fingers found the rumpled papers he kept there. Tire receipt. Ticket stubs. Then something smooth and metallic. She frowned. What was that? She curled her fingers around it and pulled a round metal object out. She could only stare. A key. What the heck was Linc doing with a…a…a hotel-room key? Her stomach dropped. Oh, God. She had to blink several times to clear her vision. Was that why he'd been so distant? Was there someone else?

Then she read the name engraved on the metal disk. Risky Business. She laughed. Five years later, the memory of that hotel still amused her.

They'd gone on vacation for Linc's birthday one year

and hadn't bothered to make hotel reservations. They weren't planning on anything spectacular, nor had they planned on a high-school soccer tournament in the town where they stopped. They'd had the choice of the one hotel.

Exhausted from a day of driving, they'd taken the room sight unseen. At the threshold they could only stare at the red velvet bed and the disco ball on the ceiling. But once the lights were off, and Linc's warm body settled next to hers…

It hadn't mattered what the room looked like. They were there. Together.

And he'd kept the room key all this time.

What else was in here? She pulled out more receipts, the insurance and registration. The only thing left was a scuffed jeweler's box. She didn't have to open it. She knew what was inside.

Linc's wedding band. He'd seen too many men lose fingers around the machines, so he always took it off before each job.

Julia curled her hands around both the ring and the key, solid reminders of the past.

Saturday Morning, Forty-One Hours Underground

THE SILENCE WAS UNGODLY. No one spoke for what seemed ages. Linc could hear their ragged breaths as if the very mountain that entombed them breathed with them. He closed his eyes, finding the dark behind his eyelids more comforting than the false night of the closed chamber.

"What the hell happened now?" Though Robert spoke softly, his question boomed in the small space.

Linc heard movement as if someone were trying to sit up or stand more comfortably. He couldn't see enough to tell for sure.

"Bet the bit broke. Happened at Quecreek, too. They'll fix it or send down another." Gabe's weary assurances didn't do much to cut the tension.

"How…how long will that take?" Ryan's young voice seemed ready to shatter.

"Dunno. Days. Hours. Depends on if they planned for it and brought any extra steel."

"They'll have planned for it," Linc said firmly, hoping to ease the mounting stress levels. He'd seen the basic plan this mine kept on file. The rescue teams would tweak it as they learned the actual conditions. There were big differences between an explosion and a cave-in. In these hills, where the layers of stone and coal were so mixed and unpredictable, the plan could change numerous times before they even started to drill.

"How the hell do you know?" Mike's tone was as hard as the broken steel above them was sharp—and ready to cut anyone in its path.

"I've seen the filed plans and those big drills are kept on standby as part of standard procedure these days," Linc explained.

"Standard procedure?" Robert spat the words. "What's standard about any of this?"

"Unfortunately, too much." Linc hated to admit it. Hated to give Robert any more fuel for the internal fire burning him up. It was true—the mining industry was

one of the most dangerous. Men didn't just die on oc-
casion. They were dying practically daily.

All the dreams and plans Linc had had, everything that had driven him to become a mine inspector,
suddenly seemed worthless. What difference had he
made?

In the fifteen years since his father's death, what had
changed?

Not a damned thing. Men were still at risk. Still
dying.

The only ones who'd been spared were the animals,
the donkeys and the birds that had once gone down
into the mines beside the men. They'd been replaced
by machines.

But the men were still needed to operate those
machines.

Linc could feel the anger rising in his gut. He wanted
to hit something, and he hoped Robert kept his damned
mouth shut. He wasn't sure he could control the need
for mayhem that he felt right now.

He rubbed his hands over his face, knowing and un-
caring that he smeared the oily coal dust over his skin.
What was the point?

What was the point of all his work? Of his life.

He hadn't changed the industry. He hadn't given Julia
a child. His younger brother had vanished, preferring to
be a runaway on the streets than part of his family.

He couldn't hold back the hard curse word. It echoed
back at him—or maybe the others were repeating it in
a resounding chorus of frustration.

Linc's eyes flew open. Though he couldn't see, he

realized something he should have been aware of a long time ago. Oh, God. Why had he been so blind?

Was this what Julia had felt when she'd decided to stop teaching elementary school? Had her passion for the job been tainted by failure?

Like the waves of an ocean lapping against the beach, his realizations came and went. The memories of that last argument rose like high tide. It had been an argument he now knew had been a waste of precious time. An argument they'd been having in bits and pieces for months. He could still hear himself yelling.

But now he finally understood. Of course she couldn't teach the little ones. Not after losing the baby. Not after their fruitless efforts to have a child. Not after his repeated refusals to even consider fertility counseling. Why hadn't he seen that?

He'd crushed her dreams as surely as the rockfall had trapped him here.

She'd escaped the only way she knew how. To still teach, but high school instead. Older kids that wouldn't be such an immediate reminder of what she'd lost.

He hadn't been able to see it from her perspective before. He'd just seen his own anger and frustration.

Selfish, selfish bastard, he cursed himself.

"What can we do?" Mike's voice was a shadow of itself and brought Linc back to the current disaster. For the first time, Linc was thankful Ryan was here. Mike was staying strong for his brother's sake. It was a struggle, but he was surviving by the sheer will of pride.

"Just be patient and wait," Gabe said. "The best thing

we can do is stay safe and together. Makes their job easier."

"We can make a plan of our own." Linc turned toward the disembodied voices. "If they're sending down the capsule, we'll have to decide what order we're going up in."

He heard movements that sounded like men perking up. He breathed a sigh of distracted relief.

"How should we do it?" Ryan's curiosity seemed to overcome some of his anxiety.

"Injured first." Linc recalled a recent plan he'd read. "Casey's got to be able to get into the capsule and stand."

"He can't do that." Zach chimed in, frightened for his friend.

"Then we'd better figure out how to help him do it."

"Can we use our belts, maybe?" Ryan offered.

"Yeah. That might work. We'll have to strap him in. It'll be a challenge."

The silence wasn't as painful now. They had something to do, something constructive to concentrate on.

"It's our only choice." Mike seemed calmer now.

"Gabe, you'll be next," Linc said.

"Like hell."

"He's right." Robert surprised Linc by agreeing with him. "With your chest hurting like it has? None of us are willing to tangle with that wife of yours."

There was laughter all around.

"Zach, you're next. They'll expect us from heaviest to lightest."

"Nah. Let Mike go up. His wife's probably about ready to have that kid. Then I'll follow him."

Silence was the agreement. "Okay, Mike then you, Zach." Linc savored the leadership role. It helped him focus on anything but the reality of their situation.

"Then it's Robert, me, then Ryan."

That was the order the rescuers would expect. But Linc knew it wouldn't happen that way. He'd never leave the kid down here alone, not even for a few minutes. But he wouldn't say anything until the time came. They needed a concrete plan, not one that would cause more contention.

It might be the last thing Linc did to try and make this mining world he reluctantly loved better, but he would do it.

He nearly laughed at himself, hearing Julia's voice telling him to stop taking care of everyone. He swallowed the sound, not wanting to explain himself.

No, this was his. Just his.

Saturday Morning, 8:00 a.m.

JULIA KNEW SHE'D DOZED a couple of times in the past couple of days, but had no idea when she'd last slept. She hadn't let herself slip into anything remotely close to that level of disconnection.

But sitting here in the cab of Linc's truck, his things and his scent all around her, she was tempted to give in to oblivion. She knew she needed to rest, but despite her heavy eyelids she fought it. Fought the fear of waking up and finding out that this was still real.

The ring box she'd found in the glove box was as warm as the rest of the truck.

She pulled out the ring, slipped it onto her thumb and curled her fist over it. It might be the only thing she had left of him.

She leaned her head back on the seat, closing her eyes. She felt brittle, as if the slightest noise could break her. A breeze could carry the bits of her away. She fought to hang on. She ached for arms to hold her and found only herself.

"There she is." Missy's voice startled her. Julia groaned, wanting to sink down onto the floor of the truck and hide. If she'd had more energy, she might have.

Julia looked out the window just as Missy opened the passenger door. Tricia stood behind her. Both of them looked as haggard as she felt.

"You okay?" Tricia asked cautiously. She had a little more sense than Missy. Age did that to a person.

Julia nodded. "Yeah. Just looking at stuff."

Tricia lifted a plastic grocery bag. "Me, too. I went to Zach's locker." Tears glistened in the woman's eyes. "If he gets out, he ain't ever going back underground."

Julia understood completely.

"I...I was just—" Julia lifted her hand. Tricia would know what the ring was. What it meant.

Their eyes met and Julia knew she'd never encountered a more kindred soul. Would their friendship survive even if their men didn't?

"Can we join you?" Missy's voice was small, and as soon as Julia nodded in invitation, Missy climbed up.

She crawled over the stick shift and settled next to Julia. Tricia settled in the passenger seat, the door closing loudly behind her.

The silence was comforting, like the sunshine that streamed through the windshield. They all faced the glass, looking past the chips in the windshield at the double-wide trailer in front of them. The office was now all but abandoned as the work crews had moved closer to the mine.

Tricia had cleared out Zach's locker. Linc didn't have a locker. This truck was his locker. There was nothing left for them here.

"I wish we could take off and just keep going," Julia said.

"Like Thelma and Louise," Tricia added.

"And Missy?" Missy provided with a tentative smile.

They all smiled and Julia didn't feel so alone anymore.

"What's stopping us?" Tricia asked.

"I couldn't find Linc's keys. Mine are at home. Linc probably still has his in his pocket." Her voice broke. She'd yelled at him so many times when she found them in his pockets or the laundry, or worse yet, at the bottom of the washing machine.

"Zach's notorious for always leaving junk in his pant pockets. The worst are the fishing lures. We've killed more than one washer that way."

"Thank God." Julia laughed. "I thought it was just us."

The camaraderie grew. She opened an eye and

glanced over at Tricia. Missy had fallen asleep. In that instant the girl's head canted and she lay comfortably on Julia's shoulder. It felt good.

"She's too young," Tricia whispered.

"Aren't we all?" Julia asked.

"Yeah."

"Thanks."

"For?"

"Coming to find me. It helps. I was slipping into a not-so-pretty place." She couldn't say much more.

"Anytime."

Warmth came from more than the sunshine, and Julia closed her eyes to savor it. For just a moment

CHAPTER FIFTEEN

Saturday Evening, Fifty-Two Hours Underground

WITHOUT THE COVER of the incessant grinding of the drills, another sound burst out of the darkness. A terrifying sound. Linc sat up, and he heard the others move, as well. Robert switched on his light, its beam weak.

"Shit!" Robert stood and moved to the flap of the shelter. "We've got water."

They'd been religiously pounding on the pipe and checking the water level until a couple of hours ago when they'd all succumbed to their exhaustion and fallen asleep.

"How fast?" Gabe's words were weak.

"Too fast." Robert stepped out of the shelter.

Linc stood and hurried after him. They moved down the slope to where they'd placed the marker, but couldn't find it. It was completely submerged.

"Something gave way. Either a wall or a pump." Robert stepped closer to the water's edge, shining the light back and forth, but the beam was too dim to see far.

"How much time?" Linc asked, his fear strong. Robert might have an attitude, but Linc trusted his judgment underground.

"A couple of hours, tops. We can slow it down some by building a few more barriers. But that won't stop it."

"We need all the time we can get."

They grabbed two more of the canvas battices and stretched them across the mouth of the chamber. They anchored them in place with rocks and scrap pieces of metal. Occasionally they had to stop and rest. More than two days with little food and diminished oxygen had sapped their energy. Linc knew the only things keeping either of them still standing were adrenaline and fear.

When they were finished, Linc could barely catch his breath and the rubbery sensation in his limbs masked any pain.

The canvas was holding, but the water was already lapping at the base of the first barrier.

"Come on." Robert laid a hand on Linc's shoulder. "Let's get back."

They were only a few feet up the incline when they heard the grinding start again. The drill was back in operation. "Thank God," Linc breathed and he saw a smile on Robert's face.

"Let's just hope they move faster than that." Robert tilted his head toward the rising water.

Inside the shelter, the others huddled together. Looking at them in the dim light, Linc realized just how worn out they all were. They wouldn't last much longer. He settled back into his spot just as Robert's lamp finally gave out. That left only the one light.

"We put up two barriers. It'll hold for a while," Linc explained.

"They'd better drill fast." Ryan's voice shook.

No one spoke after that, but there was no silence. The drill continued overhead and if he listened, Linc could hear the rushing of the water beyond.

He fought the heaviness in his chest and glanced at the meter on his belt once again. Watching it did nothing to keep the readings in the safe range, but he checked it regularly, nonetheless. He wanted to curse, rant and rave, but didn't have the energy.

The rattling sound of a wet cough broke the quiet. The kid. He was trying to be quiet, but already his body was reacting to the lack of oxygen.

That ventilation shaft had better get through soon or Linc wasn't sure if they'd be worth saving.

He knew the dangers of methane down here. They all did. No one who worked in a mine ignored that particular training lecture.

The sounds of their shuffling bodies and uneven breathing filled the air. He heard it along with the erratic beat of his own heart. His body was struggling, as well.

He didn't want to die here, like this. He knew there was nothing he could do about it, but that didn't make it any easier to accept.

He'd prayed more in the past couple of days than he had in the past ten years. Probably not since his father's death.

Did he even need words?

Wasn't it clearly written all over his soul? His wants, his dreams and deepest desires? They pulsed in his bloodstream even now with less oxygen to keep them alive.

But dreams didn't have an expiration date, did they? He sure hoped not. He still had too many waiting to be realized.

He'd almost drifted to sleep when he heard a loud crash. The drill broke through, startling them all. Linc jerked and covered his head with his arms. Rocks fell somewhere, he could hear them, but he didn't feel anything landing on him.

"It's out there." Robert still sat by the shelter opening and peered out the flap with the meager light of the remaining lamp. "I can see the drill."

Everyone cheered, their voices hoarse, but strong with renewed hope.

As quickly as it came down, the drill head vanished. There was still a distant grinding sound that Linc knew was for a second, bigger hole. But the initial shaft for ventilation was through. He breathed a sigh of relief. The fresh air would make a huge difference, both to help them breathe and to provide pressure that would hopefully hold back the water. The whoosh of the forced air was a welcome sound that drowned out the rushing water.

Still, they had to wait.

Minutes passed slowly. Finally, a tangle of wires and equipment emerged through the small hole.

"Hey," Robert yelled, not giving any chance that they'd not be heard. "We've got one injured and one with chest pains. So get your butts down here quick. And send some batteries and water. We're nearly out."

There was no response, and none was expected. The equipment was designed to find them. To listen. Not to answer.

It didn't matter. The grinding continued. That was message enough. They were still coming for them.

Linc prayed the final hole would be done soon. When the water reached the top of the first barrier, the rush nearly wiped out the second. They shored it up but knew it was temporary. Very temporary.

Saturday Morning, 11:30 a.m.

JULIA AWOKE WITH A START, not knowing when she'd fallen asleep or what had woken her. The length of the shadows outside told her it had been a while. Whatever had disturbed her hadn't bothered Missy or Tricia. She heard it again. A man's yell. His excitement cut the air and tore apart her lethargy.

"We're through. We found them." Randy ran up to the driver's-side window and pounded on it. The others awoke and Missy stared at her brother as if not understanding what he was saying. He was smiling, so it meant the men were alive, right?

Julia's breath caught in her chest, a weight she couldn't dislodge. "They found them?" She looked at Tricia, needing reassurance.

"Yeah. That's what he said."

"Let's go!" Missy shoved them. All three women scrambled out of the truck and ran up the hill.

Julia stopped at the crest and looked over the valley.

Tricia and Missy continued on, following Randy down the hill.

A watery sun fought valiantly to break through the clouds, but shadows crept over the ground between Julia and the brightly lit tents. She watched the men come and go. Watched the trucks of equipment move around. Were they even accomplishing anything? Patrick Kelly stepped out of a door then paused a moment. He hung his head and she saw him rub the back of his neck—to ease the tension, she supposed. She couldn't help but see the strain that settled over him.

He headed toward the family tent, his steps slow and purposeful. Suddenly, another man, younger this time, burst from that same door. He ran over to Patrick and grabbed his arm. She watched as they both turned away and ran back inside.

Julia was halfway across the lot before she even thought about moving. Something was going on and she was pretty sure it wasn't good, or at the very least it wasn't something she'd learn about soon. She couldn't stand waiting one minute more.

She reached the door and yanked it open. Noise and heat assaulted her senses. She realized she wasn't actually in the entry to the mine, but in a small room that was packed with men, equipment and wires. Everyone was talking at once. No one even seemed to notice her.

"The families know we had taps." Patrick's voice broke through the din. "If I tell them about this, we'll have a madhouse on our hands."

Julia shifted so she could see Patrick. He stood with

his hands on his hips, staring at a computer screen. She inched forward, trying to see what he was looking at.

"You have to tell them." The younger man with a pair of headphones dangling from his neck spoke.

"That's not what I meant. We will tell them, but we have to find a way to get this to them." He pointed at the screen.

"That's impossible. What if we see something…you know…"

"Like dead bodies?" Patrick asked so softly Julia almost didn't hear him. No one bothered to answer.

Julia felt the life drain out of her. No. The men couldn't be dead. *Linc* couldn't be dead. Not possible. She wasn't ready for that. She must have said something or moved in a way that caught Patrick's attention. Both men turned and stared at her. She moved again without thinking.

She reached Patrick's side and finally saw what they were talking about. "A camera? You have a camera down there?" she nearly screamed.

Patrick's hand clamped on her arm, not painfully, but tight enough to keep her from running and telling the others. Or to keep her from fainting; she wasn't exactly sure which he expected. She didn't really care, she wasn't doing either.

"You can't say anything," Patrick warned her.

She hoped he wasn't expecting her to respond. She couldn't speak, much less run and share the news with anyone else. She couldn't even manage to force her eyes from the screen.

She watched, mesmerized, as the camera moved

down through a dirt- and rock-lined hole. She registered the uneven cut of the walls. Vaguely, she heard a voice talking to her. Linc? No. It was Patrick, speaking gently as if trying not to spook her.

"We've already sent the microphones down. They're feeding an optic borehole camera now. We're picking up sounds. We just aren't sure what they are."

She swallowed. "Okay," she whispered, doubting anyone could hear her over the noise in the room. She didn't really care. She wasn't leaving now, not physically, not mentally.

"We're almost there," the young man said. "Shhhh...." What were they doing? Listening for something? What did they expect to hear? To see? She strained her ears. Nothing came to her. Everyone in the room had quieted. Only the hum of the computers broke the silence.

Then, faintly, she heard it. Muted male voices. *Please. Please. Please. Please.*

The tiny light on the end of the cable led the way and broke through into a pool of pure darkness. Then nothing.

"Hey! Hey, can you hear me?" A voice? A man's voice came through the computer's speakers and echoed from the headphones still dangling from the young man's neck.

Julia's knees gave out, and she felt Patrick settle an arm around her waist to hold her up. He didn't let go and when she realized he wasn't going to drag her away, she relaxed a little. She couldn't speak to thank him.

Suddenly a hand appeared on the screen. She squealed

and jumped. Cheers erupted around her. "We got 'em," the young man beside her yelled.

"Don't get your hopes up," Patrick whispered in her ear. "We might have found them. But they're still trapped." He was trying to keep her on an even keel, she knew that, but she wanted to hit him for stealing her relief and joy. The men were alive. Really alive. Not just anonymous taps from nowhere. Not crushed beneath tons of rock.

The hand on the screen moved away and only the darkness remained. Then suddenly a face appeared on the screen. *Linc!*

Did she scream his name out loud? She didn't know. She didn't care. She nearly fell this time, and knew that the only thing keeping her up was Patrick's strong arm. She touched the screen. She could almost feel the rough texture of his chin, where the grime was thick and the whiskers dark. He'd never looked so beautiful.

She ran her finger over his bottom lip, feeling the cold, hard glass and aching to touch the soft, warm skin.

"Who's up there?" A voice she didn't recognize came through the speakers.

Julia stared at the small computer screen. Linc's face filled most of it. He seemed to move even closer as if somehow that would take him up through the fiber-optic cable. If only it could.

For an almost imperceptible moment, his eyelids fluttered as if in relief. What was he thinking? How was he coping? She wanted to shout that she was here, that she wasn't leaving, but she knew he couldn't hear her.

His eyes closed again, and he backed away from the camera. He couldn't see her, she knew, but she found herself trying to conceal her emotions. He seemed to be struggling, as well, but she couldn't tell what was going on.

And then she remembered that long-ago afternoon in high school. Linc had come out of the gym from boxing practice, looking beaten and abused. She'd been in the hall, getting ready to leave, and stopped to look at him. A bruise had marred his left cheek and a white butterfly bandage sat rakishly over his eye. He'd been much the same then. Trying to hide his emotions. Always strong, always tough.

He'd called her Fancy Pants and teased her that day. Back then, all the girls had a crush on Lincoln Holmes. Her included, though she'd have never admitted it. They'd been so close and she remembered wishing he'd kiss her. He hadn't.

Now he stepped away from the camera and she felt a similar disappointment. Mike Sinclair's face appeared on the screen, but not nearly as close. She could still see Linc in the background. She watched him hungrily, afraid that if she looked away he'd disappear. She wanted to beg him to come back. She wanted to watch him until they were all rescued, as if that would somehow keep him safe.

Linc turned and his back was to her. His shirt was rumpled and tugged loose from his coveralls. Mud was smeared all down his legs. Her gaze moved back up, clinging to his image, creating a final memory—just in case.

"How's Rachel?" Mike yelled into the microphone. "Tell her I'm trying to get there."

Julia heard the words, but still didn't look away from Linc's image. With his back still to her, he leaned on the rough wall, stiff-armed, his head bowed. She realized his shoulders sagged.

He stepped backward, the shadows reaching out for him, engulfing his face, his torso, his legs and finally even the boots he wore. He was gone.

"Where did he go?" She grabbed Patrick's arm hard.

"Get us the hell out of here." The voice sounded vaguely like Linc's, but scraped on her nerves like that of a wounded animal lost somewhere out in the night.

Julia thought she heard footsteps. Where was he going? Then she realized it wasn't Linc's steps, but other family members coming into the tiny room. There wasn't enough space for them all. Noise came with them, and Julia felt the heat and claustrophobia wash over her like a wave. She stumbled. Patrick caught her before the floor did, and pulled her toward the door. She fought him, clawing at his arm, trying to get back to the screen.

"Shhh…" Patrick pulled her roughly into a hug. This man who'd been a stranger only a couple of days ago was comforting her, trying to ease the fear that threatened to destroy her sanity.

"Don't give up. Not yet."

"Why not? He's trapped down there. He's—"

"He's alive," he snapped. "Don't forget that."

"But—"

"No. Don't."

Julia realized this was the first time another man had held her since she'd married Linc. Her father had never been affectionate when she was a child. The sense of comfort was almost foreign. It gave her strength—but it wasn't enough. It wasn't Linc.

She looked up at Patrick, and with a nod, stepped away. "I'm sorry." She didn't know what she was apologizing for, so she searched for an excuse. "For losing it there. I don't normally."

"These circumstances aren't quite usual."

She almost laughed and wiped at her eyes. She kept backing away.

Outside, the cool afternoon air wrapped soothingly around her. She looked up at the cloud-drenched sky where the ever-present floodlights glared at her. And smiled a bittersweet smile.

She was still in love with Linc. She hadn't ever stopped loving him. Or wanting him. It had just got lost somehow.

A warm ache grew in her chest. She realized that all those things she'd loaded in her car were going back to where they'd come from.

She couldn't leave him. Ever.

She loved him.

Now he just had to live long enough for her to tell him so. She couldn't stop the sob that tore through her. *Please.*

It seemed like hours before the families gathered again in the tent, though Julia's watch told her it had been less than thirty minutes. She had to shove her way inside.

Patrick Kelly and the mine CEO, Martin Halston, stood at the makeshift podium. She hadn't seen Halston since that meeting at the gym. He looked like hell. Good. He needed to be as stressed as they were. He'd always been a fire-breathing dragon. Now all she saw was a withered puff of smoke.

The crowd's noise was unbearable. She looked around for her parents and Jace. She saw them across the tent. She met her father's gaze but knew she couldn't get to them. Her mother stood on tiptoe to smile encouragingly at her. Her dad gave the thumbs-up sign.

The microphone squealed just then, slicing through the cacophony like a sword.

"Please." Halston held up his hands. "Please," he repeated. "We have lots to tell you."

The crowd obliged, hanging on his every word. Needing to hear.

"Now that we've made contact with the men—"

Cheers filled the air and Halston struggled to regain control. Patrick finally put his fingers between his lips and let loose a whistle that hurt Julia's ears.

"As you know, the first drill, the air passage, broke through just a while ago. The big drill's been fixed and the second shaft is over halfway there. We believe they are all alive. But we've got at least one with injuries and another with chest pains."

The crowd sobered, and Julia struggled to hold back tears. She wasn't even sure whether they were happy or sad. Was Linc one of the injured? He'd looked fine in that brief instant on the computer screen. She turned and found Tricia beside her. They clasped hands. Missy appeared on her other side, holding on just as tight.

Shirley's face was pale. She looked stricken.

"Gabe's had heart problems," she said. Shirley's daughter had yet to arrive. Trouble getting a flight and the weather had kept her away. Now Shirley was the one here alone. Julia and Tricia stepped apart and each slipped an arm around the older woman. She refused to give Shirley the lying platitude that Gabe would be okay, but she would give her all her support.

"We've spoken with the crew that's used this equipment before," Halston explained. "Once we finish breaking through with the large bit, the men will be brought to the surface slowly, one at a time. We'll bring those who are injured or at risk up first. The men below know the plan and will make that determination. Once the injured are out, we'll bring the rest up, heaviest to lightest."

"Ryan will be last." Rita buried her face in her husband's shoulder. "He's the smallest."

Where did Linc fit into the list? Julia didn't want him up first, that would mean he was hurt. But she couldn't bear the wait if he was near the end.

"I hate that rule," Jack complained. "That means my boys come up last." His anguish was too strong. He sounded ready to shatter.

"It's a small capsule." Patrick stepped forward. "Anyone large may need help getting in and closing the hatch," he explained.

Jack nodded, though the agony on his face didn't fade.

Raymond, Julia's father, asked the question everyone was thinking. "How long will it take to get them up?"

"Ten to twenty minutes each. We can't hurry. It's like a diver surfacing from the ocean. We don't want any complications from the pressure, like the bends. There are still risks."

Patrick didn't elaborate and no one asked. There wasn't room for any more worry. It would be an eternity. Seven men, twenty minutes each.

Hours more waiting.

Saturday Evening, Fifty-Three Hours Underground

FINALLY, THE BIG DRILL crashed through.

Linc breathed in the oxygen that was coming down, tried to concentrate on what needed to be done.

"They'll send down a metal cage," he explained. The men all stood around the hole, peering up at what seemed like a very small opening, but a way out, nonetheless.

"Will we fit?" Zach didn't sound at all sure.

"It'll be tight, but yeah." Once, in a training exercise, Linc had stepped into one of the capsules. At six feet, he was tall, but thin. He'd felt like a sardine. Some of these guys were broader than him. It would be worse for them.

Moments later, the cage came down. And not empty. Food, water bottles and batteries sat in a pack on the bottom.

"What's that?" Ryan pointed at the pile of leather coiled on the floor of the capsule.

Robert leaned forward first, then Linc. "Safety

harness," Linc explained. "To belt anyone in who can't stand by themselves." Every one of them glanced over at Casey.

Linc dreaded the task ahead. While Robert replaced the batteries in their headlamps, the rest of them headed to the injured man.

They couldn't tell how much Casey understood. The man had been in and out of consciousness for the past twenty-four hours.

Zach, who knew him best, was worried for his friend. "We have to move you, buddy," he explained. "We're gonna be real careful, but it'll hurt. Sorry." Zach's voice broke with his regret. He gave his friend some fresh water and now that the lights were brighter they could all see his injuries, his cracked lips and pale skin.

"'Kay," was the weak response. They all gathered close.

Robert and Zach hefted Casey to his feet, one man under each arm. A thin cry of pain escaped, then Casey's head lolled forward. The men hurried to the capsule as quickly as they dared.

Ryan stood behind the cage to steady it while Mike and Linc wove the harnesses through the metal bars. One for under Casey's arms. One for his waist and a final one around his thighs to keep his legs from moving.

Even unconscious, Casey seemed to know he needed to keep his weight off his injured leg.

Zach finished closing the buckles, then latched the door. It was incredibly tight. Casey's shoulders were hunched and his head down. There wasn't room for any movement, which was a good thing considering his injuries.

"See you up top, buddy." Zach pounded on the cage to signal they were ready, and within a few seconds, the capsule lifted into the air, disappearing up the black hole in the roof.

"Holy cow." Ryan stared up, then they all did. His light beam reached several feet above them but there was only darkness beyond.

Linc shivered. He'd give anything if there was another way out. But there wasn't. He knew it. Swallowing, he put that out of his mind. Already his gut churned with the idea of the claustrophobic space.

"We've got some time to wait. Here." Robert handed them each a bottle of water and a plastic-wrapped sandwich from the pack that had come down. Rather than go back into the shelter, they sat where they could find dry ground.

The sandwich tasted good, but sat heavily in Linc's stomach. However, the fresh water eased the discomfort in his belly. Linc knew the bad air, lack of food and anxiety combined to make him nauseous. "Too bad they didn't send down some Jack Daniel's," he said.

"Yeah, that would have been good," Ryan agreed.

"Oh, come on." Mike nudged him, and Ryan slipped off the rock where they'd perched. "You've never had whiskey."

"Have too."

"Really? When? Mom's gonna love hearing about that."

"You shut up."

"Now, boys…" Gabe said and his fondness for them came through. Along with a tightness in his voice.

"You hurtin', old man?" Robert asked.

"Yeah. Some. I'm all right." He was obviously lying.

Linc leaned his head back against the cold wall. Gabe needed to get up top quickly, but everyone else looked fairly healthy. Ryan and Mike were still teasing each other. Zach was relaxed now and even Robert had a faint smile on his face.

Linc tried, and failed, to ignore the black hole over their heads. How was he ever going to get into that cage?

"Don't think about it. Just do it." Robert's voice broke into the panic that threatened to paralyze him. Linc turned and looked at the man who had proven strongest in this ordeal.

"That what makes you able to do this job every day?"

"Partly. But I like my work. Gets in your blood."

Linc chuckled. "I must have the wrong blood."

CHAPTER SIXTEEN

Saturday Evening, 7:00 p.m.

JULIA STOOD STARING at the television someone had
finally brought in. The reports had been too negative
and inaccurate before. But Patrick had to do something,
and taking the family members to the rescue site was out
of the question. The compromise had been the TV with
a live feed from the local affiliate. The mayor wanted
his town to benefit from the national media frenzy, so
only local reporters were allowed close enough to get
the exclusive stories.

The politics drove Julia nuts. She didn't care how
or why, she just needed to see what was happening.
The result was that the families remained out of the
way.

But the men were coming up. That's all that mattered.

She watched as the cameras panned the valley. More
clouds had rolled in. Huge floodlights had been set up
and it looked like the high-school football field at homecoming. She smiled. *Homecoming.* That's what it would
be when Linc appeared.

She chose to ignore her worries about how they'd

bridge the gap that had been between them before the cave-in.

The huge drilling rig sat at the center, its tower shooting high into the sky. Dozens of men gathered around it. While the rescue crews were no longer needed to help search, not a man had left. Familiar faces, covered in mud, stared at the drill shaft as if they could make it go faster.

The local news anchor looked out of place in his clean white shirt and dress pants. At least he wasn't wearing a tie and someone had found him a pair of rubber boots. In his deep, booming voice, he announced that the first man coming up was Casey McGuire.

Linc wasn't the man who was hurt. Julia nearly sank to the floor with relief.

"There's no one here for him." Tricia's voice cracked around the words.

Jace, who stood beside Julia, looked over at her. "What do you mean no one?" he asked.

"No family," Tricia explained. "His parents are gone and he broke up with his last girlfriend months ago." She twisted her hands together. "He practically lives at our house on his days off. He's part of us."

Julia watched Tricia's indecision, then saw her dad, Walt Robinson, step up.

Before he could speak, Jace did. "I'll go with him. You stay here with Tricia." He shook Walt's hand and there was no missing the relief and respect in the older man's eyes.

"You sure?" Walt asked.

"Oh, yeah." Jace turned to Julia. "I'll meet you and

Linc at the hospital." He shocked her with a brief hug before turning back to look over at Raymond and Eleanor. They stepped forward, into his vacant spot, figuratively and physically.

Julia watched her brother-in-law, once a stranger—and now perhaps a friend? She could only hope at this point. Maybe with family here, Linc would understand…

She refused to complete the thought. So much in their marriage had to change and part of it was her thinking, her wishing.

Jace left the tent and headed to the parking lot where his bike still sat. Despite the noise of all the machinery, she heard the roar of the big engine and listened until it faded down the road to the hospital.

"Oh, I hope Casey's not too badly hurt." Tricia didn't bother to hide her tears and her father pulled her close, letting her cry on his shoulder yet again.

The television announcer was speaking again. "The next man will be Gabe Wise, the chief of this ill-fated crew."

"Oh, I just knew it was his heart," Shirley cried, grabbing her purse and jacket.

"Don't borrow trouble." Mamie's hand shook as she patted her friend's shoulder while they hugged.

"He's alive," Julia reminded her and tried to force a smile as they embraced. "He's almost home."

"Thank you," Shirley said to Julia and held on tight for a minute before dashing out the doorway.

Julia turned back to the television. The waiting ate holes in her stomach.

Saturday Evening, Fifty-Three Hours Underground

CASEY WAS UP AND GABE WAS on his way to the surface, packed tightly into the capsule. None of them knew how long it would take to reach the surface. Linc guessed about fifteen minutes, a thought that made his gut spasm, but no one knew for sure. Linc would be last, so he'd be down here another hour and a half. Minimum.

Sounded short. Felt eternal.

The extra batteries that had come down with the cage helped chase away the shadows. The panic and claustrophobia Linc had fought so hard were relegated to the deep recesses of the mine. But they still lurked there, ready to pounce.

Just another hour and a half. Just ninety minutes. He made himself take a couple of easy breaths. They were getting out. He'd be going home. Soon.

The rising water only made the air colder, and Linc could feel the damp seeping up from the ground. He shivered as the chill soaked clear through him.

The men scooted together, hoping for some type of body warmth. He could feel the others shivering, as well.

"This sucks," Ryan said through chattering teeth.

"So tell me about it," Mike automatically replied.

"I just did."

Old habits die hard, especially brotherly one-upmanship. Linc tried to smile even though his lips felt frozen. Laughter was beyond him. It took too much energy. He let his eyes close, no longer able to fight the drowsiness.

He knew he was dreaming.

Home. He was home. First back in his mother's kitchen before his dad had died. The smell of oregano in his mother's spaghetti sauce mingled with the remnants of her perfume. She always spritzed just a bit on before Dad came through the door each night.

Then he was back in college. The night he and Julia had first made love. The tang of the pine grove they had hidden in engulfed him, then faded as her sweet scent filled him. Her shampoo smelled of flowers as he buried his face in her hair, taking part of her deep inside his soul.

She faded away, and he struggled to hold on to her. And then she was there…

In the kitchen…. The dish soap making bubbles in the air. She was yelling… Angry…

"Hey." Mike nudged him. "Drink some of that water. You're fading. You okay?"

"Yeah." Linc sat up and scrubbed his hand down his face, trying to wipe away the fear that had almost swamped him. He couldn't seem to shake the images from his mind, as if he wasn't quite convinced they were getting out of here.

His subconscious clung to the memory of home. But he knew it was a defense mechanism. He was pretending there was a home waiting for him.

What if there wasn't?

He'd spent more than two days clinging to the hope that Julia would be waiting for him up there. But was she?

His mother's kitchen had become an empty shell of a

place where he'd found her crying in the middle of the night after his dad's death.

The kitchen where he and Julia had once made love had eventually turned into a battleground.

Would he be going back to the house, to that kitchen, alone?

His stomach roiled, and his claustrophobia seemed nothing compared to this.

He'd left home on Thursday morning convinced he and Julia were on their way to divorce.

What if they were already there and he couldn't do anything but face the fallout when he got to the surface?

Would it have been easier for them both if the cave-in had just ended it all in the first place?

Linc shot to his feet. *No.* He wasn't a quitter. She was worth fighting for. *They* were worth fighting for.

"Where you going?" Ryan asked and fell into step beside him.

"Crazy—wanna come along?" Linc repeated an old saying of his dad's.

Ryan laughed, and they walked a little farther into the shadows where all his fears lurked. He wasn't hiding anymore.

They reached the water's edge. It was up at least another three feet. The second barrier had given way and the water lapped at their boots. There was no stopping it now. Being rescued was their only escape.

"We're getting out of here, kid, and you're never coming back down, you hear me?" Linc acknowledged to himself that Julia had been right. This kid had no business down here. He might not be able to put it in his report, but he could do this for her.

Ryan simply nodded as they both stared at the rising water.

CHAPTER SEVENTEEN

Saturday Evening, 9:00 p.m.

THERE WERE ONLY THREE families left. Julia and her parents, the Sinclairs and Mamie, who waited patiently as Robert came up next. The old woman looked pale, tired and nearly done in. Hank had joined them and was waiting for the go-ahead to whisk her off to the hospital in his squad car. Julia half expected the woman to be admitted along with the men. She was strong in spirit, but three days of unrelenting stress had taken its toll on her physically.

Rita was no longer crocheting. It was too close now. Her needles and yarn were packed away, ready to grab as soon as Ryan appeared. Rachel had gone with Mike while both Sinclair parents had remained here for Ryan. Ryan would be the last one up and neither Jack nor Rita would leave each other to face the long wait alone.

Julia sat. Then stood. Then sat again. Her mother paced nervously and her father sat stoic, silent, watching her. Moments later, Julia heard the roar of the crowd in the valley and the echo of the sound through the TV. They all watched Robert's ascent.

"There's my boy." Mamie's voice broke and she smiled through her tears.

"Let's go see him." Hank put the walker in front of her and grinned. The rattle of the walker was a bit slower than it had been, but just as enthusiastic.

Mamie hugged everyone then was gone. They'd meet again soon. Everyone promised.

Linc would be next. Julia moved right up to the TV and sat beside Rita. They clasped hands. "I look forward to seeing Ryan back in class," Julia said.

Rita simply nodded and squeezed Julia's fingers.

The news reporter stepped in front of the camera. Behind him, the rescue capsule was still poised above the hole. "What are they waiting for?" Rita demanded. Jack leaned forward and turned up the volume.

The reporter answered her as if on cue. "The crew seems to be spending a bit more time with the last man."

Before the reporter could say more, Patrick's frantic voice cut through the airwaves. "Get it down! Fast. That water's gonna get 'em."

Julia's heart leaped into her throat.

"Damn." Jack stood and paced.

"Oh, hurry, hurry," Rita told the TV. They watched the crew scramble to get the metal cage back down. Julia didn't remember the cable moving that quickly before.

Water was not good.

The world Julia had known just a few weeks ago was gone. Blown away by a rockfall. Buried beneath a mountain of stone. Perhaps forever.

The doubts she'd spent the past few days ignoring leaped at her with a ferocity she couldn't ignore.

Even if Linc survived the cave-in, would he survive

the slow rescue? Was he even alive now or was all this effort for nothing? Had the water flooded the chamber?

Oh, God, please don't let all this be a waste.

What would she do if he were gone from her life? Would she ever know if he still loved her?

Divorce was just as much a threat as the mountain. What if they saved him and he came back up and still told her goodbye? The thought flirted with the edges of her sanity.

Then, as if carried on the breeze, calm settled over her. She'd rather lose Linc to divorce than death. At least then she'd know he was alive. Not permanently, irrevocably gone. Just the idea of a world without him in it was beyond her comprehension.

She knew that if she had to, she would let him go.

But she hoped she didn't have to. She didn't want to. Her love for him was as strong as ever and she didn't want to lose what they had together. She had to show him it was still there.

Finally, minutes…hours later, the winch stopped as it had five times before. It had reached the bottom. Julia could envision Linc climbing into the capsule. Ryan would help him. She wrapped her arms around her waist. *Hurry. Please hurry.*

The signal was given and the winch pulled the thick cable. For long minutes it moved slowly. Suddenly it stopped moving altogether. Men jumped off the rig and from the edges of the hill. Two EMTs hurried from where the two remaining ambulances sat.

The shadows danced in the huge floodlights like

moths caught in a giant flame—back and forth, men scurried about. The reporter must have moved away as there were no voices to match the gestures and lips she saw moving.

Time ticked away. Julia had to force herself to stop looking at her watch.

Finally, the crowd moved back and the cable moved— but was it going back down?

"No! What's wrong?" Then, as if hearing her words, the cable stopped and reversed direction. Finally, the top of the capsule appeared and slowly emerged.

Ryan's face was a black mask of dirt beneath his hard hat. Water poured out of the bottom of the capsule.

No! Where's Linc? Julia trembled, her heart pounding so hard it stole the air from the room.

Rita bounced to her feet and headed to the door. "My baby," she said several times. Jack moved more slowly, obviously torn between his wife and wondering what had happened to Linc. He stared at Julia, then at her parents, who looked as shell-shocked as she felt.

"Go, go." Julia pushed Jack's shoulder. "I'm going, too." And before anyone could argue with her, she gathered her jacket and headed toward the tent opening. She had to know what had happened. Linc was down there and no one was going to keep her from him.

CHAPTER EIGHTEEN

Saturday Night, Fifty-Four and a Half Hours Underground

DRY GROUND WAS FADING FAST. Even the tiny spot Linc sat on was soggy and muddy.

He'd sent the kid up in his place. The boy had argued at first when Linc told him how it was going to go. If it had been anyone else—like Robert—Linc might not have won the argument. But Ryan was scared and cold and too damned young to be down here. Linc had more than told Ryan, he'd made him swear he'd go back to school and at least think about college.

Ryan had hesitated, but not for long. When the capsule came down, he'd looked at it so longingly, Linc hadn't even had to insist. They'd shaken hands like men, but then Ryan had stepped forward and given him a brief hug. "Hurry up, okay?"

"I'll do my best, kid." He'd relish the memory of that moment for the rest of his life.

Even if it was a short life. He scooted back, but the water licked at his steel-toed boots with a wicked slapping sound. He swallowed and prayed they'd hurry.

All too soon, he could no longer sit as the water rose to his knees. The area where the capsule came down was now flooded and he cringed. Thankful for the extra batteries, he flashed the light over the water. Waiting.

He moved and the sound of paper crackled in his pocket. He reached in and pulled out the haphazard note he'd tried to write Julia. He'd forgotten about it when the drill broke through, but now, looking at the water, he bit his lip. It was still rising. Fast.

He might not make it. Fumbling in his pockets, he found the pen he'd used earlier. His hands shook with the cold and his emotions. He had to let her know.

I'm trying to get to you. I love you. He underlined the last three words. Twice.

He sloshed around the chamber, looking for something to protect the note. Even if they couldn't get him out alive, they'd find his body and someone would give her the note. They had to.

The sandwiches had been wrapped in plastic. The old bucket they'd tossed the wrappers in floated over by the high ground. He pulled a bag out and struggled to get it open. Finally, he stuffed the paper in and resealed it. Scrunching it, he put it in his shirt pocket, then settled back against the wall to continue waiting. His thoughts grew disjointed.

Was this what his father had gone through? This dark cold…only without the hope? Linc swallowed his grief.

As a kid, he'd blamed his father for the accident, for not coming home. For all their misery.

But getting to know these men, men he realized were much like his father, he saw how unfair he'd been.

If he'd been able to, Jim Holmes would have come home.

"I'm sorry, Dad," Linc said to the darkness. "I'm so sorry."

There was no answer and he didn't expect one. But the peace that settled over him eased a lifetime of anger. He closed his eyes and pictured his father standing with his mother in a bright light. It felt right.

He didn't see Jace there, though. He wanted to find him. Had he heard about this? Linc knew he needed to make things right, for himself, for Jace and for their parents.

The sound of the capsule rattling its way down the shaft brought him back to reality. Relieved and desperate to escape, Linc shoved his way through the water toward it, his teeth banging together as he shivered. Until he saw the sky above him, he wasn't banking on anything.

Taking a deep breath, reminding himself this was just like a first plunge into a summer pool, he stepped into the deeper water. He wasn't sure if the battery would work if it got wet, so he took the light off his helmet and held it aloft.

The heavy capsule bobbed with the waves of his movements. Only the top quarter of the capsule was out of the water. It was enough.

He reached it and tried to unfasten the latch. His fingers were stiff with the cold and he fumbled. The metal tore his skin, but he barely felt the pain of the cut.

He pulled the door open and stepped inside. The cage swung awkwardly and nearly spilled him out. He gulped a mouthful of the brackish water before righting himself. Slapping the helmet and its light back on his head, Linc curled his fingers around the mesh to hold himself in place.

Reaching out, he grabbed the door and fought the water to pull it closed. He had to twist around in the tight space to get it firmly shut. He struggled with the latch. He stopped and took a deep calming breath. *Focus. One step at a time.* He concentrated on his fingers, forcing them to do his bidding. Finally, the latch clicked tight.

He scarcely had room to move and had no clue how the other, much larger men had fit in this thing. But they had. Thank God, they had.

Linc pounded on the roof and barely felt the impact. His fingers were useless from the cold. He leaned against the side of the metal cage.

He knew from watching the others that it rose into the opening cut just inches wider than the cage. Black earth completely surrounded him.

Closing his eyes, he chose not to watch.

Saturday Night, 9:30 p.m.

HAD SHE MISSED LINC COMING UP? The reporter hadn't said his name. There wasn't anyone around to tell her what was going on anymore. She'd seen Patrick on the TV screen in the huddle of men around the winch.

If Linc had come up…he'd be with the EMT crews.

"Where are you going?" Her father caught her at the doorway and touched her arm. She looked up at him, surprised. She'd nearly forgotten her parents were here.

Guilt swept through her. Despite the past, they'd been so supportive through this.

"Linc was supposed to come up before Ryan. Where is he?"

"I don't know." Her father's concern for her seemed to include Linc, which pleased her.

"Honey, wait here. They'll come tell you what's going on." He didn't sound convinced of that and she wasn't either. No one was headed this way.

"I can't. Thank you for being here. It's been a huge help." She closed the few inches between them and put her arms around him. "Thank you, Daddy," she whispered. Then she pulled back and her mom was right there, too. "You two are awesome."

"You and your young man aren't so bad, either," Eleanor admitted with a forced smile, and slipped an arm around Julia.

Their sentiments were real. Julia saw the sincerity on their faces. But they were also trying to guide her back to the seat by the TV. Away from the edge of anxiety.

The TV reporter's voice interrupted them. "From what I can see, the crews have determined that the chamber where the men have spent the last three days has completely flooded. The young man who just came up appears soaking wet from head to toe with water running from the capsule. The fate of the last remaining man is unclear."

"No!" Julia screamed. She stumbled, then righted herself. On the screen the crew behind the reporter sent the capsule back down the hole.

"Shut your mouth." A familiar voice came from out

of the camera range. Patrick. His shoulder appeared and the reporter disappeared from the screen.

There was no stopping Julia now. The reporter's words only made the worry and wait worse. She had to see for herself what was happening.

She knew that if the news was bad, she would be left up here until the mine officials figured out what story to tell her.

She couldn't wait. Agony spurred her to move, and she ran to the entry of the tent. This time, no one tried to stop her. Instead, her parents followed her outside.

Julia ran out into the woods and to the trail she'd walked so many times in the past three days. Halfway down the hill, she stumbled over the tree root she'd cursed days before. Her hands and knees hit the trail, and she swore at the mud and rocks that scraped her skin.

Her momentum kept her going, and she tumbled several more feet before the thick undergrowth stopped her.

She wanted to curl up right there and let the pain take her. She let loose a single sob before she pulled herself together. Julia might want to die with Linc, but she wasn't about to give up yet.

She crawled to her feet and ran as fast as she could manage on the terrain, no more interested in caution than before.

She broke into the clearing and shoved her way through the crowd of workers. They all knew who she was and parted to let her through.

She heard someone screaming Linc's name and realized it was her. She nearly tumbled again just as she reached the crew surrounding the hole. A pair of strong hands grabbed her shoulders, not to stop her, but to steady her. She looked up to see Patrick's familiar face. So many times during this ordeal this man had been the bearer of bad news. Now he grinned along with the rest of them.

"Almost home," one of the men operating the winch yelled.

The top of the capsule appeared above the hole. Like a mother giving birth, the earth released her final captive. The metal cage emerged into the bright lights, water gushing from the bottom of the capsule. Linc covered his eyes against the glare.

He was so close. She needed to touch him. To know this was finally real.

Before they'd even opened the door, she was pushing forward, sobbing his name.

"Let them get him out so he doesn't fall back down." Patrick said patiently. Reluctantly, she stepped back, leaning on Patrick.

The cage door opened and two men helped Linc step out. A gurney was positioned just inches away and they led him toward it.

His steps were awkward but then he looked up. "Julia," he cried and despite Patrick's hold, she launched herself at him. She slid down through the muck and into his arms.

They both stumbled, grasping for each other. She didn't care that she was soon soaked through with the

icy water he was drenched in. She breathed in the damp,
dirty smell of him and relished it. He was alive. And
here. Finally.

She cried. All the tears she'd denied for so long
rushed forward and down her cheeks.

His arms pulled her tight. "Hey, babe. I'm okay."
Something like a laugh came from his throat. "I *am*
okay."

"I'm not." She hiccuped and clung to him. "I love
you, Linc."

"I love you, too. We've got another chance. I'm taking
it." His lips were frigid, but they were alive and urgent
on hers. Somewhere along the way, she realized they'd
sunk to the ground and she kissed him back.

Cheers went up all around them and everyone high-
fived and clapped each other on the back. Linc's hold on
her tightened and he kissed her as he never had before,
as if he never intended to stop.

Julia pulled back. "Thank God." Tears blurred her
vision.

"Okay, folks." A new voice held laughter. An EMT
stood grinning at them. "Let's get you checked out so
you can finish with those plans."

Julia and the EMT helped Linc settle back on the
gurney, where they slapped an oxygen mask on his face.
Six stocky miners, including Patrick, surrounded it and
carried him up the hill to the waiting ambulance.

Jostled aside, Julia trembled and tried to stumble
up the hill after them. A strong, warm hand took her
elbow.

"Come on. Don't keep 'em waiting." Her father smiled at her and helped her up the hill and into the ambulance just before they slammed the doors and sped toward the emergency room.

CHAPTER NINETEEN

Sunday Morning, 1:45 a.m. Three and a Half Hours Aboveground

JULIA SAT BESIDE LINC'S hospital bed, waiting. He'd been poked, prodded, examined and tested for what seemed like ages. The doctor wanted him to stay until morning, just for observation.

He was finally settled. The silence grew. And grew. She struggled to think of what to say. Or do. He was alive and well. Thank God! The initial shock was wearing off along with the rush of emotion that had launched her into his arms.

Now what? Linc looked big and awkward in the hospital bed. He'd cleaned up some, but the grime of the mine still clung to his hair and streaked down the edges of his face. The fresh hospital gown and the snowy-white sheets contrasted with his darkness.

She let her gaze take in his broad shoulders and the torn skin of his fingers. She wanted to cry. She wanted to reach out and hold his hand. Hold him.

"We need to talk." His words were way too loud and he cleared his throat as if adjusting the volume.

She couldn't resist anymore. She carefully put her hand on his uninjured one. She was surprised to see herself trembling and even more surprised when he turned his hand and curled his fingers tightly around hers. "I know," she whispered.

The silence returned.

"Could you…" He paused. "Would you consider coming back home?" His hesitation told her too much and echoed what Jace had shared with her about Linc's uncertainties.

She pulled her hand away, regretting the pain she saw flash on his face. Hastily, she tugged at the ring she'd kept on her thumb. "You are never taking this off again, ever," she whispered as she pushed it back on his finger.

He nodded, staring at the ring before pulling her tight against him. "Never." He agreed and smiled through the sheen in his eyes.

Home. The word wrapped around Julia like a blanket on a cold afternoon.

She pictured the mess she'd left in the bedroom and the remnants of Linc's time alone everywhere else. She blinked to clear her vision and met his eyes. "The— uh—bedroom is sort of a mess."

"I know." Linc leaned his head back and glared at the ceiling. "I just… Sorry, I made such a disaster of it." He looked at her again. "I'll fix it."

Julia smiled. She knew he meant more than just the mess. So did she. "I'll help. I didn't exactly clean up. I was halfway packed when they called."

"Oh."

"Some of my junk is still in my car." Suddenly she realized it was all there, her clothes probably wrinkled beyond recognition. "And there's lingerie all over the bedroom floor."

They held each other's gaze. Time stopped and the silence between them filled with all the emotions Julia had questioned over the past few days. She leaned toward him. She heard the mattress crackle and the sheets whisper as he moved, too.

"I love you."

"And I never stopped loving you."

She thought she heard him laugh, but the sound quickly vanished as their lips met.

He'd said the words she'd ached to hear. It felt good to say them. It felt right.

Linc's arms slid around her and pulled her to him. When the edge of the mattress got in the way, he lifted her and drew her across his chest. Her feet left the ground, and she let herself melt into him. A soft groan slipped from his chest and she pulled back, afraid she'd hurt him, but when she tried to move away, his grip tightened and the kiss deepened.

His hands moved down her back, over the curve of her butt and back up again. She slid her fingers into his hair and held his head still as she kissed him. Deep and long, the way she always used to.

She came up for air, but he didn't let her move far away. She snuggled into his shoulder and felt his mouth on the tender skin of her neck. She turned slightly, wanting to see him. Instead, she fought to keep her eyes open as he ran his tongue down her neck, to the low neckline of her shirt. His breath came quick and hot against her skin, and she almost forgot that the door to the hallway stood open.

Every inch of her burned. She wanted to be closer to Linc, to make love to him more than she'd ever wanted him before.

"Linc," she tried to tell him, but all she could manage was his name caught on a sigh.

"Does that door lock?" His plans echoed hers. She couldn't answer when his hand cupped her breast through her shirt. She moaned something that sounded like yes, but she wasn't sure.

"Lock it," he commanded. Then as his hand gently squeezed, he whispered, "Please."

She could barely stand. How was she going to make it all the way to the door? Her feet seemed to know what to do and she was suddenly there, the smooth metal lock in her hand. It seemed to turn by itself.

Her face flushed. Were they really doing this? She leaned her forehead against the cool door, her back to Linc, trying to gather her breath and her thoughts.

"What's wrong?" Linc's voice startled her, the uncertainty in it tearing at her heart.

She swallowed. The events of the past couple of days rushed through her mind, rewinding to the last time they'd talked.

The argument.

In the kitchen.

"I'm scared," she whispered. Slowly, she turned around and faced him, leaning on the door when all she really wanted to do was melt into his arms.

"Of?"

"This." She looked up at the ceiling as if there might be answers printed there. "I don't want this to just be about the fear, about what we've been through. Nothing...nothing's really changed, has it?"

She couldn't face everything falling apart again. It would kill her.

"Probably some of it is the heat of the moment," he said softly. The pause was too long and Julia started to tremble.

"But not all. I realized a few things while I was down there." Linc's voice deepened. "I understand why you changed jobs. I know the hurt I caused you—"

Julia couldn't let him take all the blame, but he held up a hand.

"Let me finish, please? Then I'll listen to you. I swear."

She nodded and reluctantly smiled.

"You're right." He swung his legs over the edge of the bed and planted his feet on the floor. After a minute, he stood and moved toward her. "Nothing has changed. I still have to go back underground if I want to make a living. You still work with kids who are going to go into the mines." He stopped a few inches in front of her and ran a hand over his face. "And you still want a baby."

Everything he said was true. She just didn't want to think about it. "What about you? Do... Do you still *not* want a baby?" She felt her heart about to break.

Linc didn't answer, and Julia wasn't quite sure what he'd say. He moved in close and ran his finger along her jaw before cupping her chin in his palm. "I want you to be happy, babe." He kissed her gently. "I'm willing to do whatever we need to to try."

Julia breathed a sigh of relief and closed her eyes so he wouldn't see the elation in her eyes. There was more. She knew him too well. "But?"

"But I need you to do something for me, too." He waited until she opened her eyes. "I need you to accept the outcome. No matter what."

"I—" She couldn't speak and looked down.

His grip tightened, not painful but determined. "Look at me."

Reluctantly she did.

"I can't change the past, babe. More than anything I wish I could." His voice cracked. "I wanted our baby. I did."

Her heart ached as she listened to him, but she knew he needed to say it, and more importantly she needed to hear it.

"It wasn't your fault. It wasn't mine, either. But I didn't do much to help, did I?"

She forced herself to meet his gaze, hoping that the stinging in her eyes would go away. "It's been…hard."

"I know. After you left the house the other night… I have never felt so alone. It…hurt."

She couldn't stay away any longer. She leaned toward him, and before he could say any more, she covered his lips with her fingers. "You promised to listen to me, too. So, listen. I know we've hurt each other. I know the past isn't going away. But you are the only man I want." She leaned her head on his chest, needing to hear his heartbeat and his breath so blessedly alive. "I know you don't always believe we're right for each other. Or that a miner's son is good enough for a mine-owner's daughter, but you are perfect for me."

"Even if…we can't have children?"

Her breath faltered. "I can live without children better than I can live without you."

She heard him gasp just before he lifted her face to his. Had he ever kissed her so gently, so sweetly? She wrapped her arms around his neck and he walked them back toward the bed. The mattress was narrow, but there were no plans to lie side by side. Still, it felt cramped. Their lips met again and the tight quarters no longer mattered.

He tasted delicious and she couldn't seem to get enough of him. She ran her fingers greedily over every inch, as if afraid the doctors had missed some bump or bruise. She found nothing but hard, warm muscles. She sighed into his mouth and reveled in the idea of being a part of him.

Suddenly, Linc moved and while he didn't let her go, he rolled to his side, trapping her between his body and the metal rail on one side of the bed.

"Julia. I never meant to hurt you." The pain returned to his face. "I…" He closed his eyes. "I need you in my life. Always and forever." He leaned down and buried his face against her neck again.

"Shhh…" She nudged him with her shoulder, forcing him to meet her gaze. "Don't ever let me go, Linc, not even if I'm stupid enough to try to leave."

"Never." Her words seemed to give him back his confidence and before she could take her next breath, he was kissing her again, this time hard and determined. She opened for him and his tongue plunged inside, deep and claiming.

As if to remind them they weren't really alone, a knock sounded on the door. "Mr. Holmes? Are you okay?"

Linc started to laugh. The sound was precious, and Julia closed her eyes to take it into her memory.

"I'm fine," he called out. "Just fine," he whispered as he kissed her again.

"I have papers here for you to sign so you can go home," the nurse persisted.

"Thanks. Give me a minute," he said, but didn't budge. He just leaned on his elbows and smiled down at Julia.

"Linc! You're incorrigible," Julia whispered. "Behave and let's get out of here."

His smile broadened, if that were possible. "That sounds good. Really good."

It didn't take Julia long to straighten her clothes and open the door. She pulled it open, half-afraid of what—or who—would be on the other side. Just the rush of the busy hospital—and the nurse who stood with a clipboard in hand and a knowing smile on her face.

Julia felt her cheeks warm but didn't explain. She simply smiled. Home. They were going home.

THE SUN WAS BARELY ABOVE the horizon when Linc threw the last of his few belongings into the bag Julia had brought him with clean clothes. The overalls had gone into the garbage, but he had his belt and some of his other equipment.

He froze as his fingers touched the cold metal. The brass plate that would have been used to identify his body was still attached to the belt. Still in place.

For another time?

He rubbed his thumb over the engraved metal. No answer came to him. The very thought of going back underground made his gut tighten, no matter what he'd told Julia earlier. The idea of finding another job tore a hole clear through him.

The door opened, and he hastily shoved the belt to the bottom of the bag. Julia didn't need to deal with that right now.

But it wasn't Julia who came through the door.

His in-laws looked haggard and tired. Guilt crept through him. They shouldn't have to be here. Not like this.

"Morning," he greeted them, not sure why they'd come. He panicked. Had Julia changed her mind and sent them to tell him… Old fears reared their ugly heads. Linc shook his head to clear it.

Raymond stepped forward and as always Eleanor moved to a chair in the background, present but not involved.

The older man paced, looking out the window then back again. He obviously had something on his mind.

"You got something to say, Raymond?" Linc waited for his father-in-law's glare and was surprised when none came.

Silence stretched out. Long. Painful. Finally Raymond

spoke, his voice thin and tired. "You remember what I told you the day you married Julia?"

"Which part? The part about how I'm not good enough for her? Or the part where you'd end my miserable life if I ever hurt her?" Memories and pain clogged Linc's throat.

Raymond stepped closer. "The last." All the old venom was gone and his eyes were red. "This is what I meant, damn it. This horror you put her through. It's not what I wanted for her."

Linc almost laughed. "If it's any consolation, I didn't either."

Their eyes met and for the first time Linc didn't see any hostility there. Just a man, tired and worried about his child.

"Linc…" Eleanor surprised him by speaking. "We…" She swallowed as Raymond turned away from them both. "We want to do whatever we can to help. Julia's our daughter and we just want her to be happy. She loves you. You obviously love her."

Linc was shocked, both by their behavior and by his mother-in-law's words.

She stood and walked over to him. "I'm sorry things haven't been better between us."

"*We're* sorry," Raymond said from where he stood gazing unseeingly out the window.

Linc didn't know what to say. He stared at Eleanor who was smiling up at him through tears. She resembled Julia, and he realized for the first time what Julia might look like as she aged.

"We're family." She put her hand on his and squeezed.

Raymond moved toward them and stuck out his hand.
"To the future?"

Linc took his father-in-law's hand and shook it.
"Yeah. Sounds great."

"We'll stop by the house later." Eleanor gave him a
brief hug and Linc watched the couple leave, pleased
that they'd come.

ALL THAT WAS LEFT TO DO was for Julia to bring the
car around and for the nurse, who insisted he *had* to
leave in a wheelchair, to wheel him out. Linc resisted
the urge to pace—barely.

"Am I interrupting anything important?"

Linc let his gaze roam over his brother, who was now
standing in the doorway. Julia had told him earlier that
Jace was here, but he was still surprised to see the man
he'd last seen as a boy. "All this time, my mind kept
seeing you as you were when you left." Linc's voice
cracked and he took a deep breath to ease it.

"You don't like what you see?" Jace arched a brow.

"No, that's not it." Linc smiled and walked to the
door. "I'll adjust." There was an awkward moment as
Linc wondered what to do, then he stopped thinking
and pulled Jace into a strong hug. "I've missed you."
Linc stepped back and Jace followed him farther into
the room. While Linc sat down on the bed, Jace moved
nervously around the room.

He saw the resemblance to their father and to the face
he saw in the mirror each morning. There were traces
of the boy Jace had been, as well.

But there were differences, too. Too many. Long,

wavy hair. Sharp lines bracketing his mouth and the lines around Jace's green eyes told of long hours in the sun.

They'd lost so much, and while this stranger was here, now, Linc didn't know how long he was going to stay. He wanted time to get reacquainted. "You staying?" Linc asked.

"For a little while." Jace leaned against the window-sill, staring back at Linc as if he were measuring the differences, as well. "Wasn't sure you'd want me to stay."

"Hell, Jace. Of course I do. Unless you have other commitments you need to get back to." Linc wanted to ask so many question, but held back. Jace had never responded well to being pushed. Look what had happened before. Linc didn't want to lose him again.

Jace shook his head. "No. Nothing special. My business can wait for now." He didn't meet Linc's eye. "You got a pretty cool lady. I remember her from before."

"Yeah. Took me a while to figure out the best things were in my own backyard."

Jace laughed and finally met Linc's gaze. "Yeah, we Holmes boys aren't always the brightest, are we?" The silence grew long and heavy. "Look." Jace moved to stand in front of Linc. "I haven't been the best brother. Hell, I'm not the best anything. Period. I'm sorry I wasn't here when…when Mom passed."

"She would have liked to see you again." Linc struggled to keep his voice even. Jace had broken their mother's heart.

Linc watched Jace swallow and knew he didn't need to be told. The younger man turned back to the window.

"Mom wouldn't have wanted to see me." He didn't elaborate and Linc didn't ask. Again, the silence stretched.

"I figured out about two weeks after I left that it was a mistake," Jace said softly, staring stubbornly at the floor.

"Then why didn't you come home?" Sadness at all they'd lost lodged in his chest.

"Pride's an awful thing, Linc." Jace finally looked up. "And at sixteen, it's hell."

"Was it so bad being with us?"

Jace thought a minute. "No. In retrospect, I realize what you and Mom tried to do. At the time I just wanted to escape. It wouldn't have mattered if we'd lived in a palace." Jace paced around the room. "I was too young to understand Dad's death. I had nightmares for years. Of being crushed. Of you being killed. Of Mom falling even further apart. I was afraid it would really happen."

"Did running away make it all disappear?" Unfortunately, Linc understood his brother too well, and ached for the boy he'd been.

"Yeah, other people, other things took its place for a while. By the time I wanted to head home, I was too drunk to know it."

The stiffness in Jace's shoulders told Linc how hard this admission was for him. Was he waiting for Linc to reject him? That wasn't going to happen.

Linc took the first step. And the second. He rested his hand on Jace's shoulder until he looked up. "I'm sorry, too. I wasn't there for you. Not the way you needed. But

I'd like us to have another shot at it." He smiled at his brother.

Jace smiled, too. "I'd like that."

The door opened then and Julia walked in. She smiled when she saw who Linc was talking to. "Jace. Are you coming home with us?" The invitation was forthright and Linc knew Julia was sincere.

Jace hesitated. "Yeah, I'll stick around a few days. But then I'll be hitting the road." He didn't elaborate. Linc didn't push this time, but he would. He wasn't letting Jace go easily this time.

And they had time. Probably not a lot this visit, but he'd take whatever he could and take advantage of the future sitting brightly in front of him.

Linc looked at his brother, then at his wife. He'd almost lost everything, but he hadn't. Julia moved to his side and put her hand in his.

"Let's go home," she said.

Both men nodded and Linc whispered, "Home."

EPILOGUE

Six Months Later

OUTSIDE THE WINDOW, gold, red and faded green leaves fell like confetti across the walk. Linc watched Julia hustle around the house, checking decorations, the snacks and back to the stove to stir something or other. It was perfect, just as they'd planned.

He leaned in the open doorway, fascinated. He couldn't get enough of her these days and the smile that lifted his lips felt good and right.

So much had happened in the past six months. Since the cave-in. Since they'd nearly lost everything. Today would be the true end to it all. They'd wanted to wait until Casey could attend. His recovery wasn't complete, but he was out of rehab and staying with Zach and Tricia.

The doorbell rang. "I'll get it," he volunteered, knowing Julia wasn't really paying attention.

Ryan and Missy arrived first, with Mike, Rachel and their new daughter close on their tail. Rita and Jack Sinclair pulled up in their truck just as Linc prepared to close the door. The wind blew and the dried leaves scratched across the walk, encouraging him to step outside for a minute.

Linc would never get tired of the open air. He breathed it in, relishing the feel of the clean, fresh breeze. He could have stood there forever, but the wind soon kicked up. He did allow himself a moment to inhale the scent of wood smoke, dust and a faint hint of damp. A new season that let the earth rest.

Oscar Hudson, the town's only mailman, drove up just then and Linc went to the curb to accept the stack of envelopes. One of the benefits of living in a small town was that everyone had the same mailman and knew him on a first-name basis. He also knew all of them.

"Having a party?" Oscar smiled as he craned his neck in curiosity.

"Something like that." Linc headed back to the porch, sorting through the stack. A postcard caught his eye. Arizona. The bright blue sky above stark red cliffs was beautiful. Jace's now-familiar scrawl wrote a few lines across the back. Jace had promised to stay in touch and this was his way of keeping his word.

The postcards that arrived every few days were a brand-new start.

The sound of a car engine distracted Linc from his thoughts, and he looked up to see Gabe and Shirley arriving, their arms laden with food they weren't sup-posed to bring. Linc shoved the envelopes into his back pocket and took a casserole from Shirley. She never arrived without a dish of one kind or another, so why he'd expected today to be different, he didn't know.

Robert's SUV pulled up to the curb. He hustled around to open the door for Mamie. The tiny, white-haired woman was dwarfed by the truck, but Robert easily lifted her and set her down. With a practiced hand, he unfolded her walker. Linc met her at the end of the walk and accompanied her while Robert parked the truck.

They'd just settled Mamie in the recliner by the fire when Zach, Tricia and Casey arrived together. The twelve-pack in Zach's arms nearly made Linc laugh out loud.

Casey hobbled in, his crutches now well-worn. He'd been fitted with his temporary prosthesis and was still unsteady. But it was good to see him standing, nonetheless.

Finally, for the first time since the fifty-four hours they'd spent underground, they were all together.

Linc hesitated, suddenly nervous. He sought refuge with Julia in the kitchen. As she turned from stirring the spaghetti sauce, he slipped his arms around her. She fitted so well in his embrace, and eagerly leaned against him.

"What's wrong?" she asked softly.

"Nothing. Just be here for a minute."

"I'm here for always." She snuggled in closer.

"Hey, you two, cut it out," Gabe called from the other room, as if he knew exactly what was going on.

Linc's laughter was infectious, and Julia rejoiced in the fact that she'd heard it more in the past few months than in years before. As he left the kitchen, she noticed the letters in his back pocket and playfully yanked them out. Out of habit, she flipped through them, knowing he'd already seen the postcard from Jace.

They were all pristine and dry. Unlike the letter she'd

found in Linc's pocket at the hospital. He'd written her a goodbye letter while he was underground and had tried to save it in a plastic sandwich bag. It had gotten wet despite his efforts and only a few snatches survived. The rest were blurs of ink. Still, she'd treasure it. A tangible reminder of what he'd survived and that he loved her.

These envelopes were nothing more than the usual credit-card offers, a couple of bills, a flyer advertising mining equipment and a business letter. She absently glanced at the return address. Fielding Fertility Clinic. Her heart stopped. *What's this?*

She tossed the rest of the stack on the table, the intriguing white envelope still in her hand. She followed Linc to the living room and stopped in the doorway. He was talking to Robert and both men were frowning. Linc looked up then and met her gaze.

Still frowning, he said a couple of words to Robert, then headed toward her. "What's up?"

His eyes searched her face, and she knew her emotions were clear in her expression. He saw the envelope in her hand and took it.

She saw him swallow hard before looking at her again.

"I don't think now—"

She put her hand on his arm. "Please." She backed into the kitchen and he followed.

After the rescue, she and Linc had talked and for a week at the cabin, they'd talked more. For the first time, they'd listened to each other and now understood. They hadn't made any concrete plans for a family, but they'd agreed to keep trying—and hoping.

"I saw Dr. Fielding a couple of weeks ago," he admitted.

"Is that…test results?"

"I already know what they are," Linc admitted. "He called yesterday. That's just the formal report."

Julia couldn't ask because her throat had closed up. They were only a few inches apart, speaking softly, and she was sure he could hear her heart beating in her chest.

"My sperm count's low. But there are some…things we can do."

"Do?"

"To make a baby?"

She tried to read his expression but was having enough trouble figuring out her own. Fear and excitement kept getting in the way. "You'd do that?"

"Yeah." He reached up and caught her chin with his hand. "I want a baby."

She swallowed hard. "And I'm okay with whatever happens," she said. Her heart pounded, reminding her of old wishes, old hurts. She slid her arms around him and he held her tight, finally kissing her.

Hoots and hollers broke them apart yet again, but not before he whispered, "We can still try the old-fashioned way, too."

He pulled away with a wink that had her face burning. She knew that if all these people hadn't been here, he'd have carried through with that promise. Right here. Right now.

The front door banged, and she heard her father

greet their guests. Julia knew her mother would be right behind him.

"Everyone's here now," Linc said from the doorway, and she turned around to see him grinning at her.

"Is it time to let your secret out?" she asked.

Linc nodded. Julia had been supportive, but even she didn't know what he had in mind. She'd gone along with all his plans for tonight, no questions asked, though she'd been dying to know.

With a deep breath, he stepped forward and grasped her shoulders, guiding her into the living room.

"Sit here." He set Julia on the arm of Mamie's recliner.

"I need to check—"

"This won't take long." Linc returned to the kitchen and she heard the fridge open. Everyone in the room shared curious glances. What was he up to?

Julia looked down at Mamie. The older woman laughed and shrugged. Finally, Linc returned. In one hand, he held the basket she kept by the sink for her linens. He'd stacked it with wineglasses. In his other hand was the twelve-pack Zach had brought and under his arm was the bottle of champagne.

"Gabe, if you'd do the honors." Linc handed Gabe the champagne. Julia watched as Linc proceeded around the room and gave each man a beer. She laughed. The men weren't having any of this "sissy" drink as Linc called champagne.

"What are you up to, buddy?" Robert grinned. He really was a handsome man, with his muscular shoulders and salt-and-pepper hair. He should smile more often, Julia realized.

"You'll see," was all Linc said. He stopped when he got to Ryan and Missy and with a grin he handed them each a soda. Ryan grumbled in disappointment as Missy punched his arm.

Finally, everyone had a drink in hand. Even Mamie consented to a small glass of champagne. Her eyes sparkled with anticipation.

"Be careful, Mom," Robert teased. "I wouldn't want to have to answer to the staff at the facility if you get drunk."

Everyone laughed. Finally, Linc managed to plant himself at the center of the group. Julia felt her heart gallop in her chest.

He'd never looked more excited or handsome—or so alive. She sent up a prayer of thanks for letting her keep him—and for all the other wonderful people in this room.

"So much has happened since last April. I know that only you, Robert, have been able to go back underground." The sacrifice had been difficult for them all. Mike and Rachel were the hardest hit, but Casey with his medical bills was a close second. Julia knew it had kept Linc awake nights worrying about these men he'd grown so close to.

"Today, I have an offer for you all. Including you, Robert."

"What?" several of them asked at once.

Linc simply grinned. "As of today, I'm the CEO and owner of Seven Bells Consulting." He looked over at his father-in-law who raised his beer in silent salute. *What were they up to?*

"My father-in-law, Raymond Alton, has offered to finance this operation. The information Robert just told me only strengthens our position. Those ceiling pins were intentionally removed. That's what caused the cave-in."

A collective gasp went up.

Robert broke the pained silence. "No one was trying to hurt us. They just got a little overzealous. The team ahead of us didn't think anyone would follow. They moved the pins to the next section, trying to cut costs."

Linc nodded. "That's where we come in. Seven Bells will train miners to protect themselves, as well as to be more aware of what's going on. Then maybe they won't remove equipment without thinking about the consequences, and if anyone else is trapped, they'll know how to survive."

The applause surprised him. When they finally quieted, he spoke again. "You all have jobs if you want them, except you." He aimed the neck of his beer at Ryan. "You're going to college first." Ryan ducked his head and smiled as Missy hugged him.

Julia raised her own glass. None of the women spoke, but the tears were eloquent enough. They drank a silent toast to themselves for surviving and to the men who were here and alive with them.

Then Linc circled the room. In a toast to friendship and survival, he clinked his own beer bottle against that of each man who'd survived with him. Like the seven taps they'd spent hours banging on that pipe, the glass pinged in the crowded room.

When he'd finished making the circuit, Linc returned to Julia's side and raised his beer. "May we never hear that sound again."

* * * * *

HARLEQUIN® Super Romance®

COMING NEXT MONTH

Available January 11, 2011

#1680 A LITTLE TEXAS
Hometown U.S.A.
Liz Talley

#1681 HER GREAT EXPECTATIONS
Summerside Stories
Joan Kilby

#1682 HERE COMES THE GROOM
Going Back
Karina Bliss

#1683 HOME TO HARMONY
Dawn Atkins

#1684 BECAUSE OF JANE
Lenora Worth

#1685 NANNY NEXT DOOR
Single Father
Michelle Celmer

REQUEST YOUR FREE BOOKS!

2 FREE NOVELS PLUS 2 FREE GIFTS!

HARLEQUIN®

Super Romance®

Exciting, emotional, unexpected!

YES! Please send me 2 FREE Harlequin® Superromance® novels and my 2 FREE gifts (gifts are worth about $10). After receiving them, if I don't wish to receive any more books, I can return the shipping statement marked "cancel." If I don't cancel, I will receive 6 brand-new novels every month and be billed just $4.69 per book in the U.S. or $5.24 per book in Canada. That's a saving of at least 15% off the cover price! It's quite a bargain! Shipping and handling is just 50¢ per book.* I understand that accepting the 2 free books and gifts places me under no obligation to buy anything. I can always return a shipment and cancel at any time. Even if I never buy another book from Harlequin, the two free books and gifts are mine to keep forever.

135/336 HDN E5P4

Name _____ (PLEASE PRINT) _____

Address _____ Apt. # _____

City _____ State/Prov. _____ Zip/Postal Code _____

Signature (if under 18, a parent or guardian must sign) _____

Mail to the **Harlequin Reader Service:**
IN U.S.A.: P.O. Box 1867, Buffalo, NY 14240-1867
IN CANADA: P.O. Box 609, Fort Erie, Ontario L2A 5X3

Not valid for current subscribers to Harlequin Superromance books.

**Are you a current subscriber to Harlequin Superromance books
and want to receive the larger-print edition?
Call 1-800-873-8635 today!**

* Terms and prices subject to change without notice. Prices do not include applicable taxes. N.Y. residents add applicable sales tax. Canadian residents will be charged applicable provincial taxes and GST. Offer not valid in Quebec. This offer is limited to one order per household. All orders subject to approval. Credit or debit balances in a customer's account(s) may be offset by any other outstanding balance owed by or to the customer. Please allow 4 to 6 weeks for delivery. Offer available while quantities last.

Your Privacy: Harlequin Books is committed to protecting your privacy. Our Privacy Policy is available online at www.eHarlequin.com or upon request from the Reader Service. From time to time we make our lists of customers available to reputable third parties who may have a product or service of interest to you. If you would prefer we not share your name and address, please check here. ☐

Help us get it right—We strive for accurate, respectful and relevant communications. To clarify or modify your communication preferences, visit us at www.ReaderService.com/consumerchoice.

HSR10R

*Harlequin Presents® is thrilled
to introduce the first installment of
an epic tale of passion and drama by*
**USA TODAY Bestselling Author
Penny Jordan!**

*When buttoned-up Giselle first meets
the devastatingly handsome Saul Parenti,
the heat between them is explosive....*

"LET ME GET THIS STRAIGHT. Are you actually suggesting that I would stoop to that kind of game playing?"

Saul came out from behind his desk and walked toward her. Giselle could smell his hot male scent and it was making her dizzy, igniting a low, dull, pulsing ache that was taking over her whole body.

Giselle defended her suspicions. "You don't want me here."

"No," Saul agreed, "I don't."

And then he did what he had sworn he would not do, cursing himself beneath his breath as he reached for her, pulling her fiercely into his arms and kissing her with all the pent-up fury she had aroused in him from the moment he had first seen her.

Giselle certainly *wanted* to resist him. But the hand she raised to push him away developed a will of its own and was sliding along his bare arm beneath the sleeve of his shirt, and the body that should have been arching away from him was instead melting into him.

Beneath the pressure of his kiss he could feel and taste her gasp of undeniable response to him. He wanted to devour her, take her and drive them both until they were equally satiated—even whilst the anger within him that she should make him feel that way roared and burned its resentment of his need.

She was helpless, Giselle recognized, totally unable to withstand the storm lashing at her, able only to cling to the man who was the cause of it and pray that she would survive.

Somewhere else in the building a door banged. The sound exploded into the sensual tension that had enclosed them, driving them apart. Saul's chest was rising and falling as he fought for control; Giselle's whole body was trembling.

Without a word she turned and ran.

Find out what happens when Saul and Giselle succumb to their irresistible desire in

THE RELUCTANT SURRENDER

Available January 2011 from Harlequin Presents®

Love Inspired®

Bestselling author

JILLIAN HART

brings readers another heartwarming story
from

the
GRANGER
FAMILY
RANCH

To fulfill a sick boy's wish, rodeo star Tucker Granger surprises
little Owen in the hospital. And no one is more surprised than
single mother Sierra Baker. But somehow Tucker ropes her heart
and fills it with hope. Hope that this country girl and her son
can lasso the roaming bronc rider into their family forever.

Look for
His Country Girl

*Available January
wherever books are sold.*

www.SteepleHill.com

Steeple
Hill®

LI87643